THE TAMING OF JESSICA

THE TAMING OF JESSICA

ELIZABETH COLDWELL

Published by Xcite Books Ltd – 2013
ISBN 9781908766250

Copyright © Elizabeth Coldwell 2013

The right of Elizabeth Coldwell to be identified as the author of this work has been asserted by her in accordance with the Copyright, Designs and Patents Act 1988.

This is a work of fiction. Names and characters are the product of the author's imagination and any resemblance to actual persons, living or dead, is entirely coincidental.

All rights reserved. No part of this book may be reproduced, stored in a retrieval system, or transmitted in any form or by any means, electronic, electrostatic, magnetic tape, mechanical, photocopying, recording or otherwise, without the written permission of the publishers: Xcite Books, Suite 11769, 2nd Floor, 145-157 St John Street, London EC1V 4PY

Printed and bound in the UK

Cover design by Madamadari

Chapter One

The coat check boy slammed Jessica up against the wall of the cloakroom, already fumbling to release his cock from his tight-fitting black uniform trousers.

'That's it,' she purred as his mouth mashed wetly against the side of her neck. 'That's the spot.'

She'd known the moment she'd walked into the club the evening would end like this, with this eager stud about to plunge himself deep into her wet pussy. Jessica always marked out her prey when she arrived. After that, it was a simple matter of claiming him as her own.

All the staff at Envied were drop-dead gorgeous. It was clearly part of the recruitment policy. From the bar tenders to the waitresses to the girls who gyrated in cages suspended from the low ceiling, any of them could have graced the cover of a fashion magazine. But the coat check boy was the one she wanted. Six foot of solid, muscular man-candy, broad shoulders and gym-honed biceps shown off to perfection in the tight black T-shirt he wore. His body on its own would have been enough to make her inner cougar sit up and growl, but it came in combination with a face she couldn't drag her gaze from. Despite the dusting of stubble on his soft, pink cheeks that, she suspected, he affected to make him look more roguish, he couldn't have been any older than 20, with long-lashed blue eyes and artfully tousled blond hair. His lips were set in a permanent pout, designed to be kissed. If he'd been born 600 years earlier, Michelangelo would have immortalised him in marble. Jessica itched to learn whether he had the kind of long, thick cock that, as far as she was concerned, would complete the perfect package.

She'd had his attention from the moment she'd shrugged off her coat to leave in the cloakroom for safe keeping while she danced. With sex in mind, she'd dressed for maximum exposure. Her gold, sequinned top was held in place by only the thinnest of halter straps, the neckline plunging down as far as her waist. At the age of 41, her breasts might be a little softer and rounder than they'd been in her 20s, but still she had no need for a bra. Unlike most of her contemporaries, she'd had no need to resort to cosmetic augmentation to keep her figure pert – or provide a boost in cup size for a husband who wanted two overflowing handfuls to play with. They might not have been the biggest but Max had always loved her tits just the way they were.

If her top was skimpy, her skirt verged on the indecent. With a hemline finishing just below the bottom curve of her bum cheeks, it offered anyone who cared to look a clear view up to her pussy whenever she climbed stairs or bent over a little carelessly. Her panties – ivory silk, with pearls stitched into the thong back – were part of the lingerie set that had been a present from Max last Valentine's Day. Funny how Max was always forefront in her mind on those occasions when she chose to go looking for hot young flesh.

Strutting through the club on her three-inch spike

heels, she'd had no shortage of men wanting to buy her drinks or dance with her. None of them held her attention for longer than a moment; she'd already decided the coat check boy would be hers, and she waved their offers away politely.

The dance floor was packed, weekend revellers moving as one to the relentless beat. She weaved her way through to the centre of the crowd, losing herself in the music, enjoying the feeling of simply letting her body move. She knew she'd be attracting even more attention as she whipped her head from side to side, long, blonde hair swishing in time to her movements, hips circling in a rhythm designed to mimic sex. It felt good to have so many anonymous, voyeuristic eyes on her as she danced, letting them look but not touch.

Sometimes, however, she allowed them to go a little further. She remembered a night, in the height of summer, when the heat had driven almost every other clubber to wear as little as she did. Her dress, made from white stretch lace, had quickly grown drenched with sweat to the point where it became virtually transparent. The atmosphere in Envied had been thick with lust and pheromones, and it had been no surprise when some man, whose face she never saw, came up behind her and started grinding his crotch against her backside. His hands cupped her breasts, kneading them and thumbing the nipples. She'd felt his cock slip into the crack between her cheeks, thick and hot even through the layers of fabric separating them. The sensation of it nudging at the puckered opening of her arse stimulated thoughts of him fucking her there, and her knees buckled at the notion. Not that she'd allow such a liberty to a complete stranger, but it aroused her to think of him unzipping himself and letting the blunt, wet head of his cock press deep inside her arse.

It didn't seem to matter that people were watching them, as he rucked up her dress almost to her armpits so his fingers could clamp round her bare tits. She hadn't bothered with underwear that night, wanting to feel what little breeze there was against her naked pussy. Almost unable to believe she'd let the man expose her in this way, she felt her pussy gush with juice, turned on by being as good as naked in front of the watching dancers. Dizzy with lust, she almost begged him to fuck her where they stood, oblivious to the greedy gaze of their audience. Only a sudden strangled groan from the man, and the feel of his body abruptly pulling away from hers, stopped her as she realised he must have come in his pants. Tugging her dress back down, she'd rushed to the ladies' room, locked herself in a vacant cubicle and frigged herself to orgasm, two fingers of one hand buried deep in her hole as she strummed her clit.

Memories of those strange hands on her body, the feeling of being displayed to the crowd, only served to further stoke her lust, which had been on a permanent boil since she'd first clapped eyes on the coat check boy. Unable to wait a moment longer, responding solely to her urgent need to be fucked, Jessica had made her way back to the cloakroom.

She'd been in luck. He was in there alone. By now, they'd be turning people away at the door, the club packed to capacity, and until dancers started arriving to collect their coats and go home, there'd be little chance of anyone walking in on them.

He'd smiled at her approach. She hadn't even needed to say a word, or hand over the numbered ticket that would assure the safe return of her coat. 'The white faux mink, am I right?' he'd said, already turning to fetch it from the rail.

'That's right,' she'd purred, impressed by his little feat of memory, 'but I haven't come for my coat. I've come for you.'

Her Adonis had glanced at her, trying to gauge if she was joking.

'I haven't been able to think about anyone else since the moment I walked in here tonight. I need you to fuck me, if you're man enough?'

Challenge thrown down, she waited for him to respond. He didn't disappoint her. Stepping out from behind the counter, he wrapped a nicely muscled arm around her. Their mouths met in a greedy kiss, Jessica relishing the feel of his full lips against her own. Her chosen studs didn't need to be good kissers for her to have a good time, but it was always a bonus if they, knew just how much tongue to use, and when to switch their attention to the sensitive spot at the hollow of her throat, nipping and teasing. This guy – and not only had she no clue as to his name, she didn't care to learn it – certainly did.

As he continued to kiss her, he unzipped his fly, reaching to free his cock. Already thick and swollen, he gripped it at the base, running his fist up and down its length as he regarded Jessica with the look of a man who couldn't quite believe his luck was in.

'Allow me,' Jessica said, replacing his hand with hers. Nothing felt nicer than to have a hard young cock in her grasp, exploring its contours, anticipating the moment when it would fill her pussy to the brim. Juice soaked her inadequate panties, and her pussy flushed with urgent heat.

Shoving a hand up her skirt without ceremony, the coat check boy pulled her panties down as far as her knees. His hand cupped the mound of her sex, and his thumb sought her clit, rolling the slippery bud in rapid circles.

'Ah, God, that's good,' Jessica moaned, the aura of control she'd displayed to this point dissolving under the lad's frantic touch. 'But I need to be fucked.'

'Your wish is my command.' Her lover spun her round so she faced the wall. Jessica braced herself with flat palms as he undid the neck bow holding her halter top in place, the shiny gold material falling down to bare her breasts. Another tug at her panties, and they were gone entirely.

She shivered at the thought of what was to come, but before he could fuck her, she had a request she simply wouldn't let him disregard. 'Condom. In my bag.'

Her clutch bag lay forgotten on the counter, barely big enough to contain the essentials she needed for her night out: phone, purse, lipstick, and a couple of condoms. Looking back over her shoulder, she watched him hunt in the bag, pull out one of the foil packets, and rip it open with abandon. Funny how some risks weren't worth taking, she thought, given that she so routinely placed everything else in jeopardy with her clubbing adventures.

With the condom in place, everything else was just a matter of time. He crossed the room back to her with half a dozen quick strides, and pulled her body hard against his groin. Splaying her pussy lips open with one hand, he used the other to guide his cock into her wet channel. A couple of hard shoves buried him as deep as he would go, Jessica crying out at the deliciously ruthless penetration. Surely someone wouldn't fail to hear the noise they made, and come to investigate?

A bassline throbbed in the distance, its muffled beat naggingly familiar and at the perfect tempo for sex. Almost unconsciously, it seemed, the coat check boy moved in time to the rhythm, hips thrusting back and forth, the rough serge of his trousers rubbing against Jessica's flesh. This was exactly how she liked it: hard and fast, with no emotion to cloud the moment. When this was over, they'd go their separate ways with no regrets. Maybe he'd brag to his friends about the older woman he'd fucked at the club, and the little trick she'd used on him that no one else had: reaching down and rubbing the thin ridge between his balls as he got closer to coming, before slipping that same finger between her own thighs to play with her clit.

If they'd had the twin luxuries of time and a comfortable bed, she could have shown him plenty more of the same, but now her muscles were tensing and his breathing was growing harsher, his strokes so rough and powerful they threatened to knock her right out of her heels. He might have the face of an angel, but his technique and appetite were those of a horny demon. It was Jessica's last thought before her world dissolved in orgasm. With a grunt, her lover announced that he was coming, gripping her tight as his cock pulsed within her.

'Well, that was fun,' Jessica murmured, as they

separated. His only reply was to shake his head, as if in disbelief. Encounters like this clearly didn't happen to guys like him – or so he must have thought before tonight.

Top securely tied in place, Jessica made sure to retrieve her discarded panties, stuffing them into her bag. In other circumstances, she might have let the coat check boy keep them as a souvenir, but they were one of Max's favourite pairs, and he'd surely notice if they went missing.

She was relieved to see her lover didn't make any attempt to ask for her phone number, or enquire whether he'd see her again. Letting a man know she wasn't coming back for seconds could so easily bruise his ego.

'Oh, just one last thing,' she said. He regarded her quizzically. 'My coat?'

'Of course,' he replied with a laugh, fetching it from the rack. Jessica slipped it on, blowing the coat check boy a kiss before leaving.

Someone pushed open the swing doors that led through to the body of the club. A blast of music hit her, but she had no desire to return to the dance floor. She'd got what she'd come for, as the pleasurable ache in her pussy testified, and now all she wanted to do was go home and enjoy a long, hot bath before bed. Max wasn't due back from his business meeting in Milan until tomorrow lunchtime. Plenty of time for her to sleep off tonight's exertions.

Stepping out on to the pavement, she looked along the street in the hope of spotting a passing black cab.

'Need a ride home?' a voice asked at her ear.

Startled, she turned to see Max, looking elegant in a

single-breasted black business suit. He must have caught an earlier flight without letting her know. Maybe he'd tried; she hadn't checked her phone, knowing she couldn't receive a signal inside Envied, and even if she could, it was impossible to talk over the volume of the music.

He didn't greet her with a smile, as she might have expected. Instead, his dark eyes were clouded, mouth set in a grim line.

'Max, what are you doing here? I thought you were in Milan.'

'We concluded our business early. I tried you at the house, and on your mobile, and I couldn't get an answer. Then I got a call from Phillip Moore, of all people, to say he'd seen you in Envied, wearing a skirt that barely covered your arse, acting like a complete tart. How do you think a man feels when he hears someone say that about his wife?'

She noticed Max didn't stop to wonder what one of his closest business associates was doing in a club like Envied. She doubted Moore had been in there with his wife. But it seemed no one looked twice if a middle-aged man disported himself in public with a girl half his age. People could be such hypocrites.

'I just came out to have a good time,' Jessica retorted. 'Surely you want me to keep myself occupied while you're away? I get so lonely when you're not around ...'

'Look, Jessica, we'll discuss this at home,' Max said, aware their raised voices were attracting the attention of passers-by. 'For now, I want you to stop making a spectacle of yourself and get in the car.'

He gestured to where his silver Bentley waited by the

kerb. Mickey Bryce, the man he employed as his driver and errand boy, sat in the driver's seat.

'But Max –' Jessica began.

'But nothing.' She'd never heard him address her in such a dominant tone before, almost defying her to argue with him. 'Now do as you're told, or there'll be consequences.'

Consequences? What could Max be talking about? Cutting up her credit cards, or worse? Sensing her husband's increasing impatience and deciding it might be wiser not to push him any further, Jessica clambered into the back of the Bentley.

Chapter Two

'So tell me, Jessica, just why did you think it would be a good idea to tell me you were going to have a mug of hot chocolate and an early night tonight?' Max buckled his seat belt with a decisive flourish, waiting for Jessica to answer.

What could she tell him? When he'd rung her from his hotel on the Galleria del Corso, waiting in the bar for his business associates to join him for cocktails and inter-company gossip, that had been her plan. But somewhere in the intervening hours, she'd felt the need for adventure build, just like an itch, impossible to ignore. From past experience, she knew the only place to scratch it was in the arms of some hot, young stud.

'I'm waiting, darling.' Her husband sounded weary, in no mood to listen to excuses. Mickey had steered the car smoothly away from the kerb, and was waiting at a red light to turn right into what little traffic passed along Oxford Street.

'Isn't it a woman's prerogative to change her mind?' she asked, hoping to divert the conversation into safer waters.

'Only if it's a man's prerogative to chastise her if changing it makes him look a fool in front of his friends.'

'But Max ...' She didn't know what alarmed her more; the fact Max refused to be mollified, or his use of the word "chastised". It held implications she wasn't entirely comfortable with.

Jessica shifted against the cool leather seat, aware that her short skirt had ridden up when she'd sat down, threatening to expose her bare pussy. Given the filthy mood Max was in already, revealing her knickerless state to him might only rile him further. She made a surreptitious attempt to tug her skirt down, as close as it could pass for a respectable level, but he must have spotted the movement out of the corner of his eye, because he snapped, 'Stop fidgeting, Jessica. And sit up straight.'

Where had this change in his attitude come from? She couldn't help but wonder. Her husband never addressed her in less than indulgent tones, and he certainly didn't bark out instructions like some fearsome parade ground sergeant major. Still, she did as he requested, her skirt rising even higher, till its hem rested on the crease at the tops of her thighs.

Mickey's eyes, reflected in the driver's mirror, shifted downward, then quickly back to the road ahead. In that moment, she knew he'd caught a glimpse up her skirt. How much had he seen? Her legs were close together, but she kept her pussy as good as hairless, visiting one of the best salons in West London for regular waxings. And though Mickey was far too professional to give any obvious reaction, she suspected he'd seen her bare, slick lips, still plump and swollen from that swift but delicious coupling in the cloakroom.

Max must have spotted Mickey taking a sneaky peek too, because he said sweetly, 'Open your legs, Jessica.'

Alarm hit her. It was as though she'd stumbled into some game whose rules she didn't quite understand, but at which her husband was an expert. 'But you told me to sit straight. I mean, it's not very decorous to –'

'Darling, when I issue an order I don't expect it to be disobeyed. If I want you to open your legs, you'll open them.'

She should keep resisting, whatever Max said about some unspecified punishment if she did, she knew that. But the part of her that thrived on public exposure, that had allowed her to be stripped as good as bare on the dance floor at Envied by a complete stranger one hot summer night, had other ideas. Almost of their own volition, her thighs lolled apart. Jessica could swear she felt her pussy lips peel apart, revealing the luscious pink cleft between them, and she caught a breath of her own arousal, musky-hot in the air conditioned car. At least her lover had worn a condom, or his seed might by now have been leaking out on to the expensive leather, unmistakable evidence that she'd recently been fucked.

This time, Mickey took a good, long look at what she was so blatantly displaying to him, all pretence of discretion forgotten. His eyes only snapped forward once more when he realised just how close he'd come to rear-ending a big, black 4x4 waiting at the junction ahead of him.

Max reached for her handbag where it lay between the two of them on the seat, unclasped it and extracted her panties. Shaking his head sorrowfully, he asked, 'Who was he?'

'I don't know what you're talking about.' Despite herself, Jessica felt compelled to keep up the charade that she'd gone out for nothing more than a few drinks and a few dances for as long as she could.

'Well, I'm assuming you had them on when you left the house. Unless you intended to flash the taxi driver, that is?'

At his use of the word "flash", Jessica once more became aware of the show she was putting on for Mickey. In the mirror, she could see his gaze flicker constantly between her bare, wet sex and back to the road. Was the sight turning him on? Was he hard in those neat, black trousers he always wore? Would he go home tonight and wank as he thought about what he'd seen, tugging his dick as he dreamt of sticking his cock between her pouting lips?

She shook her head, unsure where these thoughts were coming from. Never had she thought of Mickey in this way. The chauffeur wasn't bad looking, even if his cheeks bore the pitted scars that followed teenage acne. His brown eyes held an appealing hint of mischief, and though their relationship had been born out of the stiff formality between the boss's wife and his most trusted employee, Mickey wasn't shy about making comments to Jessica that bordered on the flirtatious. He might have been a good ten years too old to suit her extra-curricular tastes, and a bit on the rough side, but that didn't mean she couldn't, given the right circumstances, see the two of them getting more intimate …

What was she thinking? Already in obvious trouble with Max thanks to her antics in the club tonight, now she was fantasising about sleeping with his chauffeur.

The sooner they arrived home and she could free herself from this weird, sexually charged atmosphere, the better.

Max let his warm palm rest on Jessica's thigh, dangerously close to her pussy. If he moved it just a fraction to the right, the pad of his index finger would brush against her clit. She wiggled, trying to bring his fingertips close enough to make contact, her lust at simmering point from being made to display herself to Mickey and needing someone, anyone to bring it to the boil.

The moment Max realised what she was doing, he pulled his hand away.

'Oh no you don't. Though I shouldn't be surprised you're still trying to give yourself more pleasure, even after everything you appear to have done already.' He sighed. 'I can't believe it's taken me so long to realise just what a wanton slut you are.'

Jessica made to protest, before conceding Max wasn't too far off the mark. She never thought of herself as a slut, but how else could she describe her behaviour? Not that she regretted a moment of it. She'd long ago decided that, much as she loved her husband, if he was too tied up with his business affairs to give her the satisfaction she craved, she'd find it somewhere else. The plan had always been that she'd do everything in her power to make sure he never found out. A plan that had worked like a charm – until tonight.

The Bentley pulled to a halt. Jessica glanced out of the window and realised they were home.

Max released her seat belt before doing the same to his own. 'Come on, out you get.'

It took some considerable effort for Jessica to bring

her legs together and ease herself out of the car. She didn't attempt to pull her skirt down, even though most of her bottom was on display behind, and her pussy in front. At this time of night – more like early morning, she supposed – no one was awake to witness her blatant exposure. More importantly, Max hadn't told her she could cover herself, and she didn't want to incur any more of his already considerable wrath.

Her husband didn't follow her immediately up the path to their front door. When she turned back, she saw him leaning in at the driver's window, conferring with Mickey. Their voices were too low for her to hear what they were saying, and she supposed they were discussing Max's arrangements for the coming day – what meetings he had planned, and where he needed the chauffeur to take him. She noticed that once he'd finished his conversation and came striding up the path to join her, Mickey didn't immediately drive away, but she didn't find that in any way significant. The man was probably just tuning the car radio to a station he liked, rather than the smooth jazz Max insisted on listening to.

Once inside the house, Jessica made to slip off her shoes, trying to stifle a yawn. Her body ached in the pleasurable ways that follow good, energetic sex, and the thought of a hot bath before bed appealed. 'I'm going to go upstairs,' she told Max.

'Not yet you're not,' he replied. 'Not while we still have unfinished business.'

'What business? Max, I'm tired. Can't this wait till tomorrow?'

'No, it can't.' He slammed his fist against the wall, the force of his action causing Jessica to jump. She couldn't remember the last time she'd seen him so rattled; even the failure to land a potentially lucrative business contract hadn't caused him to lose his cool like this. 'You never told me who had you tonight.'

'Please, Max. Don't let's get into this.'

'Who was he, Jess? And don't tell me you don't know what I'm talking about. You leave a club with your underwear in your handbag, and that freshly fucked look on your face, and you expect me to believe you just went to dance? Tell me his name.'

She almost broke down and sobbed, knowing how much he would be hurt by what she was about to say. But he'd left her no choice. 'I can't, because I don't know it. He's just the guy who works in the cloakroom there. And yes, what we did might have been meaningless, and sordid, and all the other things you're probably going to call it, but he gave me what I haven't had from you in longer than I can remember.'

Max remained silent for so long she wondered if he would ever speak to her again. Maybe he didn't trust himself to say anything without descending into tears and abuse. For all she knew, she'd just called time on their marriage with her confession. She'd admitted to fucking a total stranger, after all; how did she expect her husband to respond?

At last, Max let out a long, weary sigh. 'I should be a hell of a lot angrier with you than I am. I'm getting the feeling he wasn't even your first, was he?'

Jessica shook her head, still not sure where any of this was leading. She hadn't expected Max's reaction to be so calm, so measured. What was he going to do; ask her to tell him how many there'd been? And what would he say when she told him she wasn't sure she could recall them all? Those hard young bodies; so willing, so delicious and, in the end, all so utterly forgettable.

'Oh darling, why didn't you tell me you needed more in the way of excitement? Maybe I could have done something about it before now. But then again, if you hadn't behaved so badly, it wouldn't have brought us to this place, would it?'

Unable to stop the words slipping from her lips, she said, 'And what place might that be, exactly?'

'Why, the one where you're going to be spanked to teach you what happens when you fuck other men behind my back, of course.'

Spanked? The very idea was preposterous. She was a grown woman, not some silly little brat in need of punishment. So why did the thought of being over Max's knee, bottom up, waiting for him to bring his palm down on her backside send heat rushing through her belly and cause her pussy lips to plump and swell? Even as she shook her head and took a step back from him, part of her knew she needed this.

He grasped her wrist, pulling her to him. Jessica made a half-hearted attempt to break free, but inside, she'd already accepted her fate. More than that, she looked forward to it.

Max dragged her through into the living room, and pulled the piano stool out from beneath the instrument he'd bought purely for show, since neither of them could play a note. She'd been thinking of taking piano lessons for a while – it might have been a better use of her time than chasing anonymous studs, she reflected, given where that path of action had led – but if she proposed such a thing now, her husband would no doubt assume she was looking for a young, male teacher who would offer more than music tuition.

He sat on the stool, spreading his thighs a little distance apart. As he never broke his grip on her wrist, Jessica was pulled down with him, finding herself being hauled into his lap. Having tucked the hem of her skirt into its own waistband, Max ran his palm over her bare bottom in a gentle caress.

'Max, please don't do this,' she begged, though it was only a token protest. He had her where he wanted her, and she couldn't help but feel she deserved to be there.

'Before we go any further, I need to know that you understand why you're about to be spanked.'

'Yes, I do, sir.' She didn't know why she'd added that last word. Somehow it felt right to address her husband in that way, as though he was her lord and master in every sense of the phrase.

'And do you regret the behaviour that has merited this punishment?'

Jessica thought back to all her wild nights in Envied; allowing herself to be stripped and fondled on the dance floor, seeking her pleasure with whomever she chose. She had loved every minute of it, but did she regret where it had led? 'Yes, sir,' she replied.

'Now, why am I not entirely sure I believe you? Jessica, if you're holding back on me, I can always bring Mickey inside to witness your punishment.'

So that was why he'd been conferring with his driver. Was the man really still sitting outside in the car, waiting for Max to call him inside? Being spanked by her own husband would be embarrassing enough, but to have

Mickey standing by, close enough to see everything as she squealed and kicked on Max's lap, her bottom turning an ever deeper shade of crimson, would be shameful beyond endurance. Still, she was almost tempted to call his bluff, just to see how he would react.

In the end, she shook her head and said, 'No, I'll never do it again, I promise. And I really can't apologise enough for sneaking around behind your back, honestly, Max.'

He fumbled in his trouser pocket, brought out his phone, and stabbed at the touch screen with a blunt fingertip. Putting the phone to his ear, he waited for the call to be answered. 'Hello, Mickey ... No, that will be all for tonight. You can go home now, and I'll see you in the morning.' He ended the call, and stuffed the phone back in his pocket.

Straining her ears, Jessica thought she caught the sound of a car engine starting up in the street outside, and the soft purr of the Bentley as it drove away. How could she have ever doubted that her husband would be true to his word?

'I wish I didn't have to do this, Jessica.' Max almost sounded genuinely regretful as he smoothed his hand over her skin, lulling her with the tenderness of his touch. 'But that wild, uncontrollable streak of yours, that urge to be fucked by anyone and everyone – it has to be tamed. Maybe you're right, maybe I'm guilty of not giving you all the attention you need, but even so, do you really need to repay me by making some kind of cuckold out of me?'

The first swat against her backside took her by surprise. Max's hand met her firm, bare cheek with considerable force. She recoiled at the sharp crack, such a contrast to the gentle caresses of moments before. Now there was no tenderness; just the need to punish, to ensure she never misbehaved in a public arena again.

Jessica found it hard to believe anything could hurt as much as that slap. She yelped as the inescapable, fiery pain seared her nerve endings. If she had been able to catch a glimpse of her bottom, she would have seen the white outline of Max's palm gradually turning crimson as blood flowed back to the area. A moment later, and she would have been able to admire its twin, proudly adorning her other buttock. Max was marking her, leaving the imprint of his fingers on her skin like his own personal brand, and though she squirmed and pleaded with him that she'd do anything he wanted, anything at all, if only he'd stop spanking her, a small, hidden part of her wanted to wear that mark with pride. She found herself yearning to be Max's in a way she never had before; when they'd stood in church and recited their marriage vows, she'd promised to obey him. All her friends had considered that wildly old-fashioned, and until tonight she'd almost revelled in disobeying him, in taking her pleasure whenever and wherever she wanted it. Now, as slap after stinging slap landed on her arse, each one sending new flares of pain through her hot, sore flesh, she was beginning to realise there was some virtue in submitting to her husband's will.

For if no one had told her how much a spanking would hurt, neither had they informed her that the pain would gradually give way to the darkest, sweetest pleasure. She was still kicking and wriggling, but now the movements were perhaps more exaggerated than was strictly necessary and guaranteed to provide him with flashes of her pussy, blossoming into arousal once more as he continued to spank her. She knew she would not be able to take much more of his treatment before she was sobbing quietly and begging him to slide his fingers into her aching sex. Not that she thought she deserved to come, but her body's needs were overriding any sense of composure.

And spanking her was turning Max on, the steady pressure of his cock against her leg an all too obvious indication of his excitement. Once he decided she'd received enough in the way of punishment, she was sure he'd free that rigid shaft and fuck her till both of them were exhausted.

Except his self-control was greater than she could ever have imagined, for a man who'd been away from his wife for days and hadn't fucked her for – how many weeks now had it been, exactly? At last, with her bottom feeling swollen to twice its normal size and her juices running freely down the insides of her thighs, she was helped to her feet by Max. She reached for his fly, wanting to bring his cock out to play, but he pushed her hand away.

'But Max, I need it. I need to come.'

'That's not your decision to make, Jessica. You don't come until I give you permission, understand?'

'Yes, sir.' Was he really denying her an orgasm, sending her off to bed with a frustrating ache in her pussy and an unfulfilled need to have his cock inside her? She couldn't believe he could be quite so cruel, yet the feeling of being controlled by him, of having no say in her own satisfaction, thrilled her in a way she couldn't explain.

Her hand was on the doorknob when he called her name. 'You took your punishment very well, darling, though this isn't the end of the matter, not by a long way. But I've been thinking about what you said, and I appreciate that my neglect of you has been partially responsible for your appalling wildness. So I'm going to arrange for us to have a few days away.'

'Really?' She was always trying to persuade Max to take a holiday, but he always claimed some pressing piece of business was preventing him from making the necessary arrangements.

'You remember Damon Barada?'

Jessica racked her brain. The name rang a bell, but Max had so many wealthy associates she sometimes struggled to tell them apart. In her experience, one self-made millionaire was very much like another.

'Well, he owns a little island in the Caribbean, and he's always inviting us to stay in his private resort. Until now, I never really thought the time was right, but now I think a spell there would do us both some good.' He glanced at his watch. 'It's too late to do anything right now, but I'll make the arrangements in the morning. I'll book us on the first available flight.'

As he wished her goodnight, Jessica gained the fleeting impression Max was withholding some vital piece of information from her, but she was too tired, and too frustrated, to give any serious thought to the possibility. In a couple of days, all being well, they would be on some paradise island, away from all the pressures of London life and Max's business interests.

Lying in bed, resisting the urge to slip a hand between

her legs and bring herself to the orgasm she so badly craved, Jessica finally brought Barada's face to mind. Ash-blond and mid-50s, with a strong, bearded jaw and weatherbeaten complexion that gave him the air of a professional big-game fisherman. He'd made his money in telecommunications, and there were at least half-a-dozen countries in the world where it was claimed you couldn't make a mobile phone call without putting money into Damon Barada's pocket. She had met him at some black tie function she'd attended with Max a couple of years back, and been struck by the man's charisma and almost overpowering air of confidence. It was a common attribute, she'd found, among men whose wealth could be counted in the billions: a belief that the odds were, and always would be, stacked overwhelmingly in their favour.

She drifted off to sleep imagining herself lying on a sun lounger, sipping some rum-heavy cocktail and watching the waves break on an unspoiled beach of soft, white sand. And in the evenings, she and Max would make long, slow love, rekindling the passion they'd let dwindle in recent months and falling in love with each other all over again. Paradise indeed.

Chapter Three

Jessica glanced around the first-class lounge, wondering how much longer it would be until their flight was called. Sitting beside her, Max's attention was focused solely on his smartphone as he checked his emails. Even now, he couldn't switch off.

Still, at least he'd been as good as his word when it came to organising their getaway. He'd called Damon Barada the following day to make the arrangements. She hadn't been party to the conversation, but, according to him, Damon had been delighted to hear they planned to visit his resort.

At Max's insistence, she had packed little more than a selection of swimming costumes, a couple of sarongs, and an evening dress. 'It's not a formal resort,' he'd assured her, 'and no one will be expecting you to wear much in the way of clothes.'

She looked up at the monitor announcing the list of departures for what must have been the hundredth time. Flying always made her anxious, even though she knew that statistically it was less risky than travelling in Max's Bentley, and the glass of champagne she'd gratefully accepted on arrival in the lounge had done little to settle her nerves. 'Oh, here we go,' she said, reaching for her carry-on bag, 'Flight 326 to Antigua, Gate 17. At last.'

Max tapped the screen of his phone a couple of times before stuffing the device in his jacket pocket. 'There's something I need you to do before we board the plane.' He unzipped his own bag, and took out a small box. 'Put this on for me.'

Wondering what on earth he could want her to wear for a long-haul flight, Jessica peeked into the box and bit back a gasp at the bizarre sight greeting her within. A butt-plug, only a little thicker than one of her fingers, made of what looked like solid steel, with a pink crystal embedded in its flanged base. Alongside the plug lay a sachet of lubricant.

'Max, I can't,' she told him in a horrified whisper. A couple of passengers had risen and were leaving the lounge, presumably to board their flight. They couldn't have a clue what Max had just ordered her to do, but if they were to look in her direction they must be able to see the embarrassed flush she could feel burning in her cheeks.

'Oh yes, darling, you can, and you will.' He brushed a finger along her throat. 'Did you really think your punishment was over after I'd spanked you? You still have an awful lot to learn about obedience, my dear, and if I tell you to stick a butt-plug in your tight little arse, you'll do it.'

She should have objected, but Max's words were igniting a blaze of desire low in her belly. It shouldn't have turned her on to be given such a demeaning instruction, but it did, and worst of all, her husband knew it.

'Hurry up and get yourself off to the ladies'. We

wouldn't want to miss the flight, now would we?'

Max gave her a pat on the bottom, and she scurried off in the direction of the lounge bathroom. Fortunately, all the cubicles appeared to be empty. She locked herself into the one furthest from the door, and took a deep breath before removing the butt-plug from its box. She'd never worn anything like this before, which was no doubt why Max had chosen one with such a slender shaft, ideal for a novice. Even so, the thought of being pegged in such an intimate fashion made her stomach churn. Aware that time was passing and their flight might be closed at any moment, she reached up under her skirt and tugged down her panties. A tell-tale dampness in the crotch gave away her excitement at submitting to Max's kinky demand, and she couldn't deny that she wanted to do this, whatever the rational part of her brain might tell her.

Tearing open the lubricant sachet, she smeared most of its contents over the plug, and the rest at the entrance to her arse. The lube was unusually thick, designed especially for anal play, and carried a cherry scent that she suspected was Max's idea of a joke, given it was her first time. Jessica was glad no one was around to see her anointing her rear hole with the cool, sticky goo.

Reaching behind herself, she pressed the tip of the plug home. It slipped in far more easily than she might have imagined, cold metal sliding up into her hot, clutching passage, and she groaned at the penetration. No more than a couple of inches long, the plug was big enough to make her aware of its presence with every movement, but not so big that it would become uncomfortable with extended wear. Though surely Max couldn't mean for her to wear it throughout the whole journey? Antigua was around eight hours away, then there was a connecting flight to one of the smaller British Virgin Islands, and a boat ride from there to Isla Barada. Once he'd satisfied himself that she had followed his instructions, hopefully he'd relent and let her take it out. Anything else would be pure torment.

Pulling up her panties and making herself respectable once more, Jessica flushed the toilet. She hadn't heard anyone come in while she'd been fiddling with the butt-plug, but it was always best to be on the safe side. Glancing at her reflection in the mirror that ran the length of the wall as she splashed water on her face, she noted the redness in her cheeks and the glittering brightness of her eyes. She'd found herself taking shorter steps than usual as she exited the cubicle, trying to minimise the movement of the toy inside her, but its very presence was stimulating her beyond belief. How foolish she'd been to think that Max's display of dominance over her had been a one-off. She only hoped he wouldn't think of trying to enforce this strange brand of discipline on her in front of Damon Barada or the guests of the resort; that would be too humiliating for words.

Taking a deep breath, she went to join Max in the lounge once more.

'That was good timing,' he said as she approached him, the smirk on his face telling her he knew just how much of an effort she was having to expend to keep her breathing, her motions, her demeanour as close to normal as she could. 'They've just made the final call. Let's not keep them waiting any longer.'

Jessica followed Max out of the lounge, heading in the direction of Gate 17. He walked at a fast pace, causing her to scamper to keep up with him. The pressure of the plug in her arse was sheer torture, and she almost begged Max to slow down. But that would have been admitting he'd won even before the game – and on one level that was all this was, just a cruel, teasing game – had properly begun. So she bit back the whimpers of frustration and need and trotted obediently after him.

They were the last two to board the plane, the flight attendant greeting them with a smile as they headed for their first-class seats and giving no indication that they'd been keeping the rest of the passengers waiting. Whatever torment Max intended to put her through, at least he was doing it in comfort, Jessica thought as she took her seat. She shuddered at the idea of sitting crammed in economy with her bottom plugged.

Nerves overtook her as the plane thundered down the runway and began its steady ascent. Even if she hadn't been a nervous flyer, she wouldn't have been able to relax, not with all her senses concentrated on the subtle but overwhelming presence of the plug in her rear hole.

Slowly, England receded beneath the clouds. Normally, she'd be in holiday mode by now, looking forward to the moment when she put on her bikini and stepped onto the beach for the first time, but already this was no normal holiday. Max was turning the pages of the in-flight magazine, seemingly oblivious to her plight. He spoke only to accept a glass of champagne for himself and another for Jessica from the flight attendant. Apart from that, she might as well have been travelling on her own for all the company he provided.

An hour into the flight, he finally addressed her. 'I want you to go to the toilet,' he told her.

Thank God, she sighed to herself. He's going to let me take this wretched thing out. His next words told her she shouldn't have expected things to be that simple.

'You will take one of the flight attendants with you. Him –' Max gestured with the corner of his magazine to the red-haired young man who was preparing a gin and tonic for the businessman in the seat across the aisle. 'You will tell him you have a problem that needs urgently attending to, and then you will show him the plug in your arse and ask him to remove it for you. If he wants to do anything else to you, you will allow that.'

'Max, what are you talking about? I'm not going to let a man I don't even know fuck me, if that's what you want.'

'Why not? It wouldn't be the first time,' Max pointed out.

He had her there. She'd been happy enough to have sex with strangers on her terms, so why should she object if Max wanted her to do it on his? And looking at the flight attendant as he bent over to hand the businessman his drink, the fabric of his uniform trousers stretching across the firm moons of his arse, she realised the guy was pretty cute. Thinking of how it might be to have his cock sliding up inside her, she felt her arse clench around the metal plug, her pussy contracting in unison.

When she glanced back at Max, she noticed for the first time how his chinos strained at his crotch, moulded tight to his erection. This whole situation – making her peg her arse for the flight, ordering her to offer herself to another man – was turning him on.

'Well, go on then, he's free,' Max said. 'Just make sure you take the necessary precautions. I can trust you to do that, can't I?'

Not quite able to believe what she was about to do, Jessica pressed the call button. Alerted by the light above her seat, the redheaded flight attendant came scurrying over.

'Is everything OK, madam?' he asked. His voice had an appealing Southern Irish lilt, and when he smiled, dimples appeared in both his cheeks.

'I – I need your assistance with something.' She had to force the words out. 'Please would you accompany me to the toilet?'

If he was startled by the request, he didn't show it. He merely said, 'Are you having some kind of medical emergency, because I can put a call out in case there's a doctor on board?'

She shook her head. 'It's nothing like that. If you come with me, I'll explain, I promise.'

The attendant glanced round, satisfying himself that no one else might need his attention in the next few minutes. Then he said, 'Lead the way.'

She picked up her shoulder bag, remembering Max's warning about taking precautions. Then she stood and made her way to the first-class toilets, the attendant following a pace behind. No one in the half-empty cabin appeared to pay them the slightest attention. She pushed open the door of the first one she came to, and ushered him inside, locking the door securely behind them.

'Now, if you wouldn't mind telling me what this is

about,' he began, but she put a finger to his lips, shushing him.

'Before we go any further, tell me your name,' she said.

'It's Darragh.'

'And I'm Jessica.' Somehow, it felt important to establish some kind of connection between the two of them. She thought of Max, sitting in the cabin, waiting for her to give herself to this man. 'And what I need you to do for me, it – it's rather intimate.'

'Really?' He quirked an eyebrow, his tone betraying his enthusiasm.

'Yes.' Her throat dried as she tried to ask him to remove the plug. Unable to form the words, she simply bent over the sink, presenting her arse towards him. The invitation was unmistakable, and she felt him flip her skirt up onto her back, then hook his fingers in the waistband of her panties. He began to edge them down, stopping as he registered the sight of the gleaming jewel protruding from her bumhole.

'What the –?'

Somehow, she found her voice. 'I've been a bad girl,' she told Darragh, 'so my husband made me plug myself. Then he made me bring you in here. He wants you to take out the plug, and – and …'

He ran his fingers over the end of the plug, the motion sending fresh, hot waves of sensation rippling through Jessica's rear passage.

'I've never seen anything quite like this,' he admitted. 'And you say I've got your husband's permission?'

'Yes. You can do whatever you want to me.'

Darragh whistled under his breath, then returned his

attention to the plug. Catching hold of the flanged end, he turned it in a slow circle, causing Jessica to cry out as it touched places inside her she'd never had stimulated before. Just that, and the feeling of being half-naked in an aeroplane toilet while a strange man played with her in such a fashion, was almost enough to have her coming where she stood. When his fingers strayed lower, to brush her pussy lips and the tight bud of her clit, he had to know that the wetness he found there wasn't just lube.

'God, you're hot for this, aren't you?' he said.

Jessica could only gasp in response, as his touch on her clit became a pinch, and a small orgasm shuddered through her. She clutched at the sink, embarrassed at how easily this man had made her come.

'Tell me what you want,' he ordered her as he toyed with the plug again, his voice a harsh rasp. The small cubicle was heavy with the scent of Jessica's juices and cherry lube.

'Please – please take the plug out of my arse,' she begged. 'And put your cock in there instead.' The words tumbled out before she could stop them.

'Anything for the lady,' Darragh said, sounding happy to oblige. Grasping the plug again, he eased it out with surprising gentleness and placed it on the sink unit, just out of her eyeline. As he unzipped his fly, Jessica hunted in her bag and brought out a condom.

'The lady wants you to use this too,' she told him, dropping to her knees in submissive fashion to pull his trousers and underwear down, and roll the condom on to his long, slim shaft. Once she had him sheathed to her satisfaction, she turned round, bending over the low toilet bowl and thrusting her rear end towards him.

'That's grand,' he murmured, running his fingers over her upraised arse. Part of her reckoned he was imprinting the sight on his memory, so he could share with his friends the story of how he'd fucked a more than willing blonde in the arse at 30,000 feet. She couldn't stop him bragging; nor did she want to. Somehow, it felt like another part of her punishment for all the times she'd cheated on Max.

For a moment, her thoughts drifted back to her husband. Would he even now be picturing what she and this handsome young flight attendant might be doing to each other? Would he ask for a description on her return, demanding every last sordid detail? Did he know how much she needed to be fucked right now?

Darragh guided the head of his cock slowly up and down the length of her slit. She could feel the heat of it even through the condom, and she wriggled her arse, wanting him to stop teasing and fill her.

Although the plug had already stretched her a little, as Darragh's crown began to inch into her arsehole she registered a marked difference in thickness. Cold metal was replaced with hot, hard flesh, and she groaned at the feel of him. Max should have been here, watching, urging the Irishman on to claim her arse, maybe even waiting his own turn with his cock in his hand.

The first stroke, shallow as it was, had her holding back a cry that threatened to alert anyone outside the cubicle to what was happening within. 'You OK?' Darragh asked, concerned that he might be hurting her.

'Yes,' Jessica whispered. 'It's just – you're going somewhere no one ever has before.'

'Not even your husband?' he asked, sounding slightly

incredulous.

She shook her head. She couldn't see his face, but she could imagine the grin that split it as her revelation sank in. Darragh cupped one of her bum cheeks in his hand, then gave it a smart slap. 'You're a bad, bad girl, so you are.' He chuckled. 'Well, I'd better make this good for you, hadn't I?'

He started to saw his cock in and out of her arse, moving to a rhythm designed to suit them both. Gripping the toilet lid so hard her knuckles turned white, Jessica surrendered to his power, the assurance of his strokes. She shouldn't be enjoying this as much as she was, but it seemed that owning up to her desire to submit allowed her the freedom to let herself be taken in ways she'd previously rejected. God, if only she'd known how good it felt to have her arse fucked, she'd have let Max do it long ago.

Behind her, Darragh was stepping up the pace, his groin slapping against her rump with every stroke. He wouldn't be able to hold back much longer, she knew, and she didn't want to be left high and dry if he finished before her. Reaching between her indecently damp thighs, she rubbed the wet knot of her clit, already feeling the first tremors of orgasm quaking in her belly.

'Oh God, oh Jesus, Mary, and Joseph!' Darragh muttered as his own climax overtook him, and Jessica couldn't help wondering if he'd one day admit to this encounter in some confessional box. Tell the story the right way and he'd have the priest green with envy, she thought. Then the tight muscles of her arse were clutching at the Irishman's shaft, and she was babbling words that didn't make any sense as she rode out the waves of orgasm.

They came back to their senses quickly, aware that Darragh needed to resume his flight attendant duties before anyone realised quite how long he'd been gone. As he disposed of the condom and eased his wilting cock back into his underwear, Jessica patted herself dry with toilet paper, then used another twist of it to wrap the butt-plug in. She let him leave the cubicle first, while she splashed her face with water and brushed her hair. Try as she might, though, she couldn't disguise the brightness in her eyes, the glow that came from having been thoroughly fucked.

When she returned to her seat, it was to see that Max had abandoned the in-flight magazine in favour of a paperback thriller he'd bought at the airport. He appeared to be engrossed in the book, but his brief sideways glance acknowledged her return.

'So, did you do as I asked?' he asked. Her only reply was to hand him the paper parcel containing the plug. He took it from her with a look that told her how proud of her he was for what she'd done.

'Can I get you a drink, sir? Madam?' The familiar Irish voice was soft at her ear. Jessica looked up, trying not to blush as her eyes met Darragh's. The flight attendant's tone might be wholly professional, but his gaze was anything but.

'Champagne, please – for both of us,' Max said.

'Coming right up, sir. And we'll be serving lunch in the next 20 minutes.' Before Darragh turned back in the direction of the galley to fetch their drinks, he added, 'I hope everything's been to your satisfaction so far?'

'Well, my wife certainly seems pleased with the

service.' Max's comment was left hanging between them as Darragh retreated, but, out of the line of sight of anyone passing by, Jessica could see him rolling the butt-plug between his fingers – a subtle reminder of what he had put her through. She couldn't help wondering whether this concluded her punishment, or whether he still had more ways up his sleeve of making her pay for her misbehaviour.

Chapter Four

The landing strip came into sight, a dark stretch of asphalt against stark white sand, and Jessica braced herself for touchdown. The remainder of their flight to Antigua had passed without incident, and there they'd transferred to this plane, big enough only for half a dozen passengers and the pilot, for the short trip to St Thomas island. From here, they would travel by boat to Isla Barada.

Max had been quiet on this flight, though whether that was down to the fact he was plotting some further act of humiliation for her or he simply got nervous travelling in a small aircraft she couldn't say. When they'd disembarked at V.C. Bird International, Darragh had waved them off the plane. 'See you again,' he'd murmured to her in among the usual bland words of farewell. If their paths crossed on the return journey, would Max give her permission to fuck him a second time? Part of her hoped he might, though mostly she wanted to keep it as a delicious one-off, just as she had with the guys she'd snared on her clubbing adventures.

She glanced around the confines of the cabin as the plane's wheels made juddering contact with the ground. The blond man squashed somewhat awkwardly into the seat at the front of the plane looked familiar, though she couldn't for the life of her remember where she'd seen him before. With his pretty, pouting looks, maybe he modelled for fashion magazines. Never mind, it would come back to her.

What concerned her more was that there appeared to be only one other woman travelling out to the island, and the unfriendly look Jessica had received in response when she'd smiled a greeting had convinced her the pneumatic blonde was no woman's woman. The way the girl hung on to what Jessica presumed to be her husband's arm, even though there appeared to be a good 50-year age gap between the couple, helped convince her of that. She really hoped Damon Barada's resort wasn't simply some kind of glorified boys' club, where Max would spend the whole week networking. He'd promised her a holiday she'd never forget, but watching him talk shop wouldn't feel much like a holiday to her.

Clearing customs at the airport was a formality, and soon the little group was climbing into the boat that would take them out to Damon's island. Thirty minutes later, they pulled into the sheltered bay closest to the resort.

To Jessica's surprise, Damon Barada stood barefoot on the beach waiting to welcome them, greeting each passenger, male or female, with a hearty hug.

'Max, lovely to see you again,' he boomed. 'And Jessica, darling, it's been far too long ...' For someone she'd only met once, he was awfully familiar in his manner, but his welcome made them feel like close friends, rather than guests.

He moved on to the next person off the boat, the

blond man Jessica recognised but couldn't put a name to. 'Hey, Sebastian, so you finally made it ...'

Jessica turned her head to look at the man, hoping his surname would come to her, but Max pressed a hand into the small of her back. 'Come on, Jessica, we've got to check in.'

He guided her up the beach, towards the low, white complex of resort buildings. The reception area had a marble-tiled floor, its coolness welcome after the fierce heat of the Caribbean afternoon. A dark-skinned girl in a white tunic dress smiled broadly from behind the desk.

When she wished him a cheerful good afternoon, Max introduced himself to her. 'Ah yes. Mr Sheringham, you're in Suite 5. I'll get someone to take your luggage.' He scrawled his signature on the printed sheet she handed him, and was given a key card in return.

'Does it have an ocean view?' he asked.

'But of course.'

When Jessica made to follow him down the corridor, the receptionist halted her progress. 'Mrs Sheringham, I'll need you to come with me – and bring your bag with you, if you wouldn't mind.'

Jessica looked at Max, but he simply gave a curt nod. 'Do as she asks, Jessica.'

With that, he was gone. Jessica hesitated for a moment, then realised the receptionist was regarding her impatiently. Having no idea where she was being taken, she followed the girl, whose black spike heels clicked briskly on the tiles.

At last, the receptionist pushed open the door of a small room that reminded Jessica irresistibly of the interrogation suites she'd seen on any number of TV detective shows, containing nothing but a plain wooden desk and two chairs. A tinted window ran the length of one wall, though Jessica couldn't seem to see what it let on to.

'If you'd just like to wait here, Mrs Sheringham, the customs official will be with you in a second.'

'Customs? But ...' When they'd gone through passport control on St Thomas, Jessica had assumed that was it for the outward leg of their journey. If extra checks were required, why wasn't Max – or any of the other passengers, for that matter – being subjected to them?

Before Jessica had time to ponder the matter further, the door opened again and a striking woman with skin the colour of caramel stepped inside. She wore a blue uniform shirt and black trousers, and her black hair was tied back in a ponytail beneath a peaked cap. More alarmingly for Jessica, she carried a clipboard and what appeared to be a pair of latex gloves.

'Sit down, please, Mrs Sheringham,' she ordered.

Meekly, Jessica did as she was told, cowed by the woman's obvious air of authority.

'I'm Officer Abrams.' As the woman spoke, she was placing Jessica's Louis Vuitton carry-on case on the desk and unzipping it. 'And you've been selected for a random bag search.' She flashed Jessica a smile, trying to suggest this was as inconvenient for her as it was for Jessica. 'I'm sure this will be nothing for either of us to worry about, and then you'll be able to begin your holiday.'

With efficient movements, she pulled item after item out of the bag. Jessica couldn't help but blush as her flimsiest, laciest panties – the ones she'd packed specifically so Max could enjoy the sight of her wearing them – were laid out on the table. At least, she thought with relief, Max had taken the butt-plug from her on the plane. How would she have explained that to this woman if it had been discovered lurking in her luggage?

Her relief was short-lived. Unzipping the pocket that ran the width of the bag's exterior, Officer Abrams reached inside and fished out what looked like a make-up case. Except she'd already thoroughly investigated Jessica's make-up collection, contained in a bag that matched the design of the carry-on case. 'Now, what do we have in here?' She opened the case, her eyes widening at the sight of what waited inside. One by one, she pulled the items out. A six-inch vibrator in black latex, designed to look like a penis, with a fat, domed head and sculpted veins running along its shaft. A tube of anal lube, the same brand as Max had given her to use with the butt-plug. And a pair of black leather wrist cuffs, lined with red faux fur.

'Come to the island to party, have we?' the customs officer. 'Tell me, Mrs Sheringham, do you use the cuffs and the dildo on your husband, or does he use them on you?'

'I – I ...' Jessica stammered. She'd never seen any of those toys before. Certainly, she had a vibrator or two in her bedside drawer, but she preferred the pocket rocket type, small, discreet, and capable of bringing her to a peak in moments, not something as crude and obvious as a fake black dick. Someone was playing a cruel prank on her. But who on earth could have placed the things in her luggage?

Then she remembered. When they had been driven to the airport, Max had sent Jessica out to the car first while he'd set the house's alarm system, and brought the luggage down to the car himself, rather than asking Mickey to do it. That would have given him plenty of time to put the bag of sex toys in her case. Maybe he wasn't playing a trick on her, after all. Maybe he'd intended that, as Officer Abrams had suggested, they could use their time on the island to play some kinky sex games together.

It was nothing to be embarrassed about, she told herself, even if the customs officer did seem to be relishing watching her squirm as she made a show of examining the vibrator in detail. They must be done here now; the case had been checked inside and out. Once it was repacked, Jessica could be on her way.

Officer Abrams gave the front pocket one last pat. 'There seems to be something else in here.' This time, she drew out an apple. 'Now, this is serious. You're in trouble, Mrs Sheringham.'

'What do you mean?' The appearance of the apple wasn't a mystery; the couple had been offered fruit as part of their in-flight meal, and Max had taken a couple of apples. One he'd eaten on the plane, the other he'd slipped into Jessica's luggage in case he felt hungry before they reached Isla Barada.

'It should have been picked up on St Thomas. We have very strict rules on bringing foodstuffs to Isla Barada, particularly fruit and vegetables. They can carry all manner of pests and diseases which could cause havoc to the island's ecosystem.

'Oh, come on,' Jessica protested. 'It's only an apple.

What harm could it do if you just ignore it?'

Officer Abrams shook her head in resigned fashion. 'I wish I could, Mrs Sheringham. But rules are rules, and you've broken them. I'm afraid you're going to have to be punished.'

'What do you mean, punished? You're going to confiscate the apple, fine me?'

'Yes, I'm taking the apple, but you're not going to be fined. Stand up, Mrs Sheringham.' All trace of warmth had disappeared from the woman's voice. When Jessica obeyed, on trembling legs, she added, 'Now strip.'

'But this is ridiculous. You can't make me ...'

'Oh yes I can,' Officer Abrams said. 'We have our own jurisdiction here, and if you're going to refuse to obey my orders, then I can simply have you deported back to the UK, with or without your husband.'

'Please, I don't want to take my clothes off.' Jessica glanced around the room as if someone might miraculously hear her plea and come to her aid, but the door to the room remained stubbornly shut. She was alone with this stern, demanding customs officer, who was already slipping on the latex gloves.

'You should have thought of that before you brought unauthorised fruit to the island, then, shouldn't you?'

Aware she could delay the moment of her exposure no longer, Jessica pulled her polka dot-patterned vest top over her head, and placed it on the table, then tugged down her skirt and stepped out of it. She looked at Officer Abrams in mute supplication, hoping she wouldn't have to carry out the instruction any further. But the officer stared back, unmoved by Jessica's silent request, and merely waited for Jessica to reach behind herself, unclip her bra, and add it to the pile of clothing. She folded her arms over her breasts, shielding them from the officer's cool scrutiny.

'And the rest,' Officer Abrams snapped.

Biting back a sob, Jessica bent down to take off her panties.

From his vantage point behind the one-way glass that gave him a perfect view into the interrogation room, Max licked his lips as he watched Jessica being forced to strip bare by the woman she completely believed to be part of the island's customs and immigration service. What Jessica didn't know was that Isla Barada had no customs and immigration service, and no policy on prohibited foodstuffs. This whole scenario was one of Damon Barada's favourite fantasies – the dominant authority figure enforcing their own brand of law on a helpless victim – and every woman who came to the resort had been put through it on her first visit, always with her husband or partner looking on and enjoying the action. Some men requested that the customs officer be played by a man, but as Jessica had already been fucked by that Irish flight attendant, Max had wanted her to be stripped, examined, and spanked by another woman.

This afternoon, Damon stood beside Max, watching the scene being played out before them. 'One of the perks of the job,' he'd said when he'd slipped into the viewing gallery moments after Officer Abrams had started rifling through Jessica's lingerie. 'And I do so enjoy watching Delice dish out the discipline to some poor girl – or, in this case, your gorgeous wife. You know, Max, I really can't believe it's taken you so long to bring Jessica out to the island. Care to tell me what finally brought this on?'

'Not really,' Max replied. He knew he was sounding churlish, but he was still recovering from the knowledge that Sebastian Voller was one of his fellow guests at the resort. The man had been waiting to join the party in Antigua, having flown from Frankfurt. Of all the people Max least wanted in his personal orbit, Voller had to be top of the list. The owner of the largest manufacturer of eco-friendly lighting in Germany, both he and Max had bid for the contract when the Mayweather hotel chain announced it was embarking on a worldwide programme of refurbishment. With over 200 hotels bearing the Mayweather name, landing the job of upgrading each one would have secured the future of Sheringham Light Sources for years to come. As it was, the contract had gone to Voller. He'd never been able to find any evidence the man had offered some kind of sweetheart deal to encourage them to accept his bid, but the rumours that Voller had done just that refused to go away. Max might have played hard, but he always played fair, and to see Voller swagger into the departure lounge at V.C. Bird airport, oozing self-satisfaction, made him wish he'd chosen any other week to visit Isla Barada.

By the time he'd shaken off his gloomy musings, Delice Abrams had already finished taunting Jessica with the sex toys he'd planted in the case. Maybe, he thought, forcing his full attention back on the scene unfolding on the other side of the glass, when he'd been planning this he should have suggested that the toys be used on Jessica before she was allowed to leave the room. The thought of this gorgeous, uniformed bitch using the vibrator on his wife's pussy, forcing her to beg for her satisfaction, had his cock rock hard in his chinos. If he'd been on his own, he might have undone the fly and stroked himself as he watched, but he didn't feel comfortable playing with himself in front of Damon. Of course, if his friend wanted to take himself in hand too, that was another matter, but all in good time.

By now, Jessica had begun to remove her clothes, with an obvious measure of reluctance. She was clearly ashamed at having to strip on the customs officer's command, and the sight of her embarrassment and confusion, coupled with her increasing nakedness, had Max hornier than he'd been in a long time.

'God, your wife's got a fucking amazing body,' Damon drawled. 'I can't tell you how long it's been since I saw a woman strip in that room who still had her original tits. Don't know about you, Max, but I can't stand those big, fake melons.'

Max didn't reply, afraid his voice would crack and betray his excitement. Jessica was edging her panties down, keeping her legs together and trying to avoid revealing her pussy to the other woman for as long as she could.

'My favourite bit will be coming up any time now,' Damon confided. 'The bit where the officer makes her bend over the table and show off everything. What do you think?'

Somehow, Max managed to say, 'When you and I first talked about – about what we were going to make Jessica do, I started picturing it, but I never thought it would be as good as this. But then I never really thought Jess would submit. I thought she'd protest, argue, ask for me, but she hasn't.'

'That's because, deep down, she wants this. Your wife's a natural submissive, you lucky bastard.' Damon chuckled. 'Which is great, because it means that, sooner or later, we're all going to get to enjoy a piece of her.'

'Well, that's not exactly why I brought her here,' Max said, finally deciding to open up a little. 'I'm trying to stop her letting other men fuck her whenever she gets the urge. I want her to be exclusive to me, to respond to my commands, bend to my will.'

'And she will, Max, she will,' Damon assured him, 'but not before she's been trained. Forgive me saying this, but you're hardly the most experienced dominant on the island, now are you?'

Max shook his head. Until the other night, when he'd caught Jessica falling out of Envied half-dressed and freshly fucked, he'd never entertained more than the faintest thought of mastering her. Whereas Damon, and most of the other men who came to the island, were serious dominants, some even going so far as to take the opportunities their wealth afforded them to live the lifestyle on a 24/7 basis. The first time he'd issued an order in anger to Jessica had been the moment he'd told her to get in the Bentley outside the club, and he had some serious catching up to do if he was to attain the level of dominance Delice Abrams was so expertly displaying at this moment.

He dragged his eyes away from the sight of Jessica spreading herself over the desk, widening her stance on Officer Abrams's command so the lips of her pussy and the pucker of her arsehole came into view. 'So what are you suggesting I do?'

'Give her the rest of the day to get used to the set-up, let her realise you haven't exactly brought her to Disneyland, then put her in the auction tonight,' Damon said. 'There'll be three other women on the block, but it's not the first time here for any of them. The guys will go wild for some fresh meat, and you'll get the pleasure of seeing the lovely Jessica being trained by an expert dom. Learn the tricks, see how she responds, and then you'll have all the fun of making her yours once you get home.' His grin widened to a leer. 'Oh, and of course you'll get to play with the house girls too. I mean, what's the point in having any number of submissive honeys around the place if you don't get to enjoy them?'

Max nodded, conceding the point. With the exception of a couple of dominant women, including Delice Abrams, who were employed for those times when a man might want to see his slave being disciplined by another girl, the female staff of Isla Barada were all supremely submissive, and more than willing to serve the guests in whatever fashion they might require. Damon really had got all this sorted out.

'OK, so why don't we get back to enjoying the show? I think Jessica's just about to undergo a thorough cavity search.'

Though her words were muted by the thick glass separating the two rooms, Max could hear Jessica's pleas as the customs officer probed between her legs with her latex-gloved hands. Indeed, he swore he could almost make out the soft squishing as two of those fingers worked their way into her wet cunt, while a third pushed into her bottom hole. Despite the embarrassing position his wife had been placed in, it was obvious to him that she was receiving pleasure from being treated in this dispassionate fashion.

Though he'd tried his best to hold back, Max couldn't restrain himself from slipping a hand into the pocket of his chinos and surreptitiously stroking and squeezing his swollen cock. He wanted to dash into the other room and sink his shaft into his wife's open, liquid channel, but that wasn't how this scene was designed to end. Delice Abrams's slender finger had strayed to Jessica's clit now, buffing it, and Jess was clutching at the table, her body wracked with visible spasms and her face contorted with ecstasy.

'She comes so beautifully,' Damon commented, his voice hoarse as he fought to suppress the extent of his own excitement. 'I can't wait to see how she'll look with the marks of a whipping on her skin.'

'So what happens now?' Max asked, as Jessica, without being allowed to dress, began to put all her possessions back into her carry-on bag.

'Well, your lovely wife will be taken to her quarters – she's sharing with Honey Forrester, I believe. As for you, my friend, I do believe a massage is in order. I guarantee it'll ease some of the stress of your journey.' Damon's broad grin clearly indicated he knew Max had a more pressing urge that needed easing. 'Let's take you to see Jasmine. I think you'll like her. She has a very talented mouth …'

Chapter Five

Almost as soon as Jessica had zipped up her bag, there was a knock at the door of the interrogation suite.

'That'll be someone come to take you to your room,' Officer Abrams told her.

'But – but I'm not dressed,' Jessica replied, unable to believe this woman intended her to leave the room naked.

'Get used to it,' was the curt response. 'Come in!' the officer called out, and the door opened to admit a white-uniformed blonde, barely out of her teens.

'Are you ready for me?' the girl asked, her eyes sweeping over Jessica's body with a look that seemed to indicate she'd seen it all before.

'Sure, May. You know where you're taking her, don't you?'

The girl nodded. 'If you'd like to follow me, Mrs Sheringham.'

Meekly, Jessica did as she was told, carrying her clothes in the crook of one arm and wheeling her luggage behind her. How had she let herself be put in this position, where she could be guided naked through Damon Barada's hotel without a word of protest? Her senses were alert for a door opening, or someone turning a corner and coming upon them; already she was conjuring up some explanation for her lack of clothing, and why the unmistakable scent of sweat and sex juices clung to her bare skin. But the corridors were deserted; no staff members, no fellow guests to witness her humiliation.

Max, she seemed to recall, had been directed up a flight of stairs to his room, so she was surprised when May came to a halt before a plain wooden door on the ground floor. The girl slotted a key card into the lock and pushed open the door.

'Here we go. This is your room.'

Jessica gained an impression of what looked like bamboo-framed bunk beds, white-painted walls, a plain wooden floor. More like a bedroom in some girls' reform school than a luxury resort complex. 'But my husband –' she began, as May ushered her inside.

'Is in one of the executive suites. Don't worry, you'll see him soon enough. Now, wouldn't you like to meet your roommate?' Without giving Jessica time for the implications of those statements to sink in, May continued, 'Honey, Jessica's here. Be nice to her.'

'Oh, you know I'm nice to everyone,' came a soft voice from the upper bunk.

Jessica watched in surprise as a woman appeared, not so much climbing down from the bunk as uncoiling herself and slithering to the floor. She appeared to be somewhere around the age of 30, though Jessica couldn't help wondering whether her firm jawline and unlined skin owed something to the surgeon's scalpel. Her glossy, waist-length black hair and the slightly upward set to her eyes hinted that her ancestry lay somewhere in the Far East. She wore a bottom-skimming white dress that clearly showed the bumps of her dark nipples and the shadow of her pubic hair beneath it, and her feet were bare. She didn't seem in the slightest bit surprised to see that Jessica was entirely naked.

'Now, let's put your clothes away,' May said, snatching the top, skirt, and underwear from Jessica's grasp almost before she knew what was happening, and making a move to take her carry-on case too.

'If you've got make-up and a wash bag in that thing, I'd take them out now,' Honey advised from behind her. Instinct telling her the woman knew what she was talking about, Jessica did as she was told. Once she'd retrieved them, May almost snatched the case from her, unlocking a small cupboard built into one wall. There appeared to be another case in there, as expensive as Jessica's own, but Jessica only got a glimpse before the cupboard was shut and locked again.

'How do I get to my clothes?' Jessica asked.

'They'll be taken out for you, depending on what you'll need. The rest of the time, you wear the dress that's been left on your bunk.' May gestured to the bottom bunk, and Jessica saw a dress as sheer and skimpy as Honey's lying on the bedcovers. It didn't surprise her to see no underwear accompanied it. 'I'll leave you two to get to know each other, then.' May gave her a polite smile, and retreated from the room.

Only when she'd gone did Jessica realise she hadn't left them the key card. Wanting to call after the girl, she went to the door, but when she tried to open it, it didn't budge. They were locked in.

'Will someone tell me what the hell's going on?'

Jessica almost sobbed, rattling the door handle in frantic fashion.

'Oh goody, a virgin,' Honey said, not unkindly. When Jessica turned to look at her, she added, 'Seeing as everyone's clearly been keeping you in the dark, why don't I enlighten you? You can put that dress on if you want, but who wants to cover up a nice little figure like yours?'

This day was getting ever more surreal, Jessica thought as she reached for the dress and pulled it over her head. She'd been plugged, fucked, stripped, probed and made to come, and now she found herself in a room with a girl who was looking at her like she'd happily get between her legs and lap up all the juices that had spilled from her as she'd orgasmed under Officer Abrams's expert touch.

'But I'll tell you what you really need before we go any further. Be a sweetheart and get the tooth mugs from the bathroom, will you?'

Opening the bathroom door, Jessica found a small room, as plain and functional as the bedroom, with room for a shower cubicle, toilet, and sink. She snatched up the glass tooth mugs that stood on a shelf above the sink, and returned to find Honey retrieving a bottle from under the mattress of the top bunk.

'Vanilla vodka,' she said, unscrewing the cap and pouring a generous amount of alcohol into each of the mugs. 'Strictly forbidden in the girls' rooms, of course, though your husband will have access to a superbly stocked minibar, and 24-hour room service if his tipple of choice isn't already supplied. I'm pretty sure they know I have this, but they haven't punished me for it –

yet.' She clinked her glass against Jessica's. 'Welcome to Isla Barada, babe.'

Again the talk of punishment. Jessica sat on her bunk, discovering the mattress was thicker and considerably springier than the thin, institutional thing she'd been expecting. She took a sip of the vodka, letting it warm her down to her belly as Honey arranged herself on the bed beside her, legs tucked under herself, and began to answer all the questions that had been buzzing round her brain since the moment she and Max had boarded the flight to Antigua.

'So, you've clearly figured out this isn't your average holiday resort ...'

'Well, when Max told me this place was the height of luxury, I really wasn't expecting anything like this.' Jessica flung out a hand, indicating the basic nature of their accommodation.

'Oh but it is, and you'll see just how luxurious it really is very soon. But all the perks, all the real treats are reserved for the men. After all, they're the ones in charge here.'

Shaking her head, Jessica said, 'I don't understand.'

'It's simple, babe. Damon Barada runs this place as a playground for men like him – rich, dominant men with submissive wives.' Honey cast her a concerned look. 'You are submissive, right?'

It was the first time anyone had posed the question to Jessica, and she considered it for a moment. The thrill she'd got when Max had hauled her over his knee and spanked her; the way she responded whenever anyone gave her an order, whether it be to take off her clothes or invite a stranger to use her however he wanted ... 'Yes,' she said at length, 'I suppose I must be.'

'Well, this is how it works. Your husband, and mine, and all the other men here, are going to use us for their pleasure for as long as we're here.'

So this was how Max was paying her back. She'd been using men for her pleasure, every time she hooked up with a stranger in a nightclub toilet or enjoyed a sweaty back alley fuck, and now the tables had been royally turned.

'Refill your glass?' Honey asked. Without realising it, Jessica had drained her drink, and now she held out the tooth mug for another shot of vodka.

'You know, you're the first person who's been kind to me since we got to this place. That horrible customs officer, she treated me like I was a piece of meat…' Jessica shuddered, and swallowed her drink. She closed her eyes as the alcohol burned through her, and when she opened them it was to see Honey grinning at her.

'Oh Jessica, you've got a lot to learn.' Honey reached out and stroked Jessica's bare shoulder, her touch light and comforting. 'And you won't get a better teacher than me, I promise you.'

Suddenly, Jessica yearned to know more about her new roommate. 'So, tell me how you come to be here?'

'Because I promised when I was a girl that I'd never make the same mistake as my mother.' Jessica was about to ask what mistake that might have been, but Honey beat her to the punch. 'I was never going to marry a man without money. I know that sounds callous, but my mother came from nothing. Her family were dirt poor, doing their best to scrape a living any way they could. My father was English. He took up a teaching post at the university in Chiang Mai, and that's where he met my mother. She worked in the canteen there. It was love at first sight, she always said.' Honey scoffed, as though she didn't believe in the concept. 'They were married two months after they first met, and when he went back to London, he took his young Thai bride back with him. Now, I'm not saying they weren't happy – they were, blissfully so, right up until the day he died – but money never stopped being a struggle for us. I grew so sick of not having the nice things lots of my friends had, of always having to scrimp and save, that I determined I would marry for money, not love.'

'So you don't love your husband?'

'Oh, I'm very fond of Ray.' Honey grinned. 'And not just because he owns a huge chunk of Soho and is worth close to half a billion pounds. The fact he likes to beat my arse black and blue with a paddle with his initials cut into it is just a bonus. And the other ladies here will tell you the same – love's all very well, but money makes it so much better.'

'Are there lots of couples here this week?' Jessica was processing the thought of being used by any number of men, as well as Honey's casual assertion that being rich was what really mattered. For her, the bonus was that Max had money; she knew she'd love him just as much if he was a poor but hard-working academic, like Honey's father had been.

Her new friend shook her head. 'No, last night there was just me and Ray, and Chester Macken and his wife, Simone. And Damon mentioned over dinner that two more couples were arriving today …'

Jessica thought of their travelling companions on the

plane to St Thomas, the pneumatic blonde and her elderly husband, and nodded.

'So that's it. But there are five or six single men as paying guests, a couple of whom are really hot, let me tell you. I've been here three times before, and I can safely say this is the best selection of guys Damon's had staying here.' Her mouth quirked in a sly smile as she regarded Jessica. 'The real question is who'll get to master you for the week.'

'Max will, surely? That's why we're here, isn't it, so he can dominate me?'

'Maybe, maybe not. Some men like to see their wife being punished by another man. It adds to their thrill. And then, of course, they can punish her later for being such a slut.'

'That hardly seems fair.'

'Like I say, babe, you've got a lot to learn. But I doubt we'll find out any more until tonight. That's when the auction happens.'

'Auction?'

'Oh, it's one of Damon's regular events. Once all the female guests have arrived, he puts them on the auction block and sells them to the highest bidder. It's quite exciting, really, not knowing who's going to buy you or how much you might be worth. But don't worry about that now ...'

Scooting closer to Jessica, Honey wrapped an arm around her and pulled her into an embrace. Their lips met, Jessica tasting the lingering remains of vodka and the unique sweetness of Honey's mouth. She expected the kiss to turn into something more, for Honey to pull her down to the mattress so she could lick and lap a trail down her body, all the way to her pussy, but it seemed for now she was just content to cuddle Jessica close. When Jessica felt her eyelids beginning to flutter shut, sleep threatening to claim her, she didn't fight the feeling. In London, it would be gone midnight now, and she'd had a long, strange day. The night lying ahead of her promised to be longer and even stranger.

Wrapped in Honey's arms, she slept, dreaming of strange men whipping her, claiming her, making her into the submissive Max clearly hoped she could be.

The sound of the door being opened jolted her into wakefulness. For a moment, she had no idea where she was, then she saw Honey's arm draped loosely over her breasts, heard the soft rise and fall of the other woman's breathing, and awareness rushed back.

'Honey, wake up,' she muttered, scrambling to sit up, 'someone's here.'

'Rise and shine, ladies.' The woman who addressed them was Officer Abrams – or had been the last time Honey had seen her. Gone was the customs official's outfit. Now she wore the crisp white dress with popper fastenings down the front that seemed to be the uniform for Damon Barada's female staff. Jessica's stomach gave a lurch as she considered the possibility that her interrogation and extended strip-search had all been some kind of kinky set-up. 'It's nearly time to get you ready for the auction. But first, a little dinner.'

She clapped her hands, and May entered the room, wheeling a trolley on which were two trays, each containing a plate covered by a metal dome, and a glass of iced water. May took one of the trays and handed it to

Honey. She took the cover off the plate, to reveal a salmon fillet drizzled in a lemon-scented sauce, a plump baked potato from which rose an appetising wisp of steam, and a green salad. At least they're not going to starve us while we're here, Jessica thought with some relief. She took her own tray gratefully; her last meal had been on the flight from London, and suddenly she had a voracious appetite.

Her own dinner consisted of a baguette stuffed with slices of chicken and avocado, a side salad studded with juicy cherry tomatoes, and a crisp red eating apple. She couldn't swear to it, but the apple looked identical to the one that had been confiscated from her luggage. It didn't surprise her. Just the latest in a long line of mind-fucks, she told herself.

'May is going to look after you. I'll be back shortly to collect you. Woe betide you if you're not ready.'

'Yes, Mistress Delice,' Honey replied. 'Of course, Mistress Delice.' Jessica wondered if she was the only one who picked up on the lack of deference in her new friend's tone.

While Jessica tucked into her sandwich, May took more items from her trolley. The two matching white robes, which she hung on the back of the door, seemed innocent enough, but when Jessica looked up from her meal to see May retrieving a long metal bar which had a leather cuff at each end, her stomach gave a lurch. Was that how the women were taken to auction, in shackles? She glanced at Honey, seeking reassurance, but her friend seemed oblivious to the whole process. That wasn't so surprising, she supposed, given that Honey had been around this particular block on three previous occasions.

Honey was the first to push away her plate.

'Mistress Delice wishes you to take a shower before you change, but be quick about it,' May told her. Without ceremony, Honey pulled her dress off over her head and tossed it onto her bunk, walking naked into the little bathroom and giving Jessica an eyeful of her pert, round bottom in the process.

As she munched on her apple, Jessica heard the sounds of water running, and Honey singing to herself, loudly and off-key. By the time she'd finished her meal, Honey was strolling back into the room, a towel wrapped around herself, which she discarded on May's command. Jessica couldn't help but marvel at how this fragile-looking girl, a good ten years Honey's junior, could issue orders which were immediately obeyed, while Mistress Delice, who seemed to radiate dominance from every pore, received nothing from Honey but thinly disguised cheek. Honey was right; she had a hell of a lot to learn about the submissive mindset.

For now, May was glaring at her with impatience. 'Get undressed, and in the shower.'

Not comfortable about stripping where she stood, Jessica took off her dress nevertheless. It seemed disobeying any order, or not performing it to a certain standard, might earn you a punishment around her, and she'd already been on the receiving end of Mistress Delice's wrath. The memory of those long, slender fingers invading her front and rear caused her pussy to clench, almost as if it wished it was still full, and she scurried into the bathroom before her body could fully respond to the thought.

The hot spray beat down on her as she scrubbed away the last traces of her journey – and all the torments she'd undergone – since she and Max had left the house that morning, from her skin. The scents of sweat, come, and cherry-flavoured lube were washed away, replaced by the faint citrus aroma of her favourite shower crème. When she stepped back into the bedroom, she felt human again.

Her sense of wellbeing took a jolt at the sight of Honey. She wore only the robe, loosely fastened around her shoulders, and her hands had been cuffed to a wide leather collar May had fixed round her neck. With her wrists pressed together between her breasts, the big, heavy globes were displayed in tantalizing fashion through the gap in the robe. The metal spreader bar she'd seen earlier had been used to secure Honey's legs about 18 inches apart; Jessica knew that would force her new friend to take short, awkward steps. She prayed May didn't have the same humiliating fate in mind for her.

She was at least spared that, though May abruptly yanked away the towel she'd fastened around herself, leaving her naked once more. Unlike Honey, she found her hands being cuffed behind her back before May fastened a collar around her neck, buckling it at her nape. The remaining robe was slipped over her shoulders. She'd have liked to apply make-up before being prepared for auction, feeling strangely vulnerable without even a coat of mascara or slick of lip gloss. The idea, she supposed, was that the men who were bidding to own her would see her as she really was, without any artificial adornment.

Mistress Delice striding into the room once more

stopped her thoughts in their tracks.

'All ready, are we?' she asked, glancing from Jessica to Honey and back again without expecting an answer. 'So let's go, they'll be waiting for us.'

Jessica followed Mistress Delice out into the corridor, wondering exactly where they were about to be taken. Honey shuffled behind her, with May bringing up the rear of their little procession. She thought she was being taken back the way she'd come from the interrogation suite, but she couldn't be entirely sure, as there was nothing to distinguish one cream-painted corridor from another. This part of the complex reminded her of any number of blandly decorated airport hotels she'd spent time in; she almost expected to glance out of the window and spot a passenger jet coming in to land.

Taking a left turn, they came to a wider passageway, thickly carpeted and with Pre-Raphaelite artworks hanging on the wall. In any other resort, she'd have expected the selection of paintings to be reproductions; given Damon Barada's vast wealth, she couldn't be entirely sure she wasn't looking at the real thing.

The change in décor indicated they'd reached a part of the building frequented by the male guests. Like the lobby she'd visited briefly when she and Max first arrived, this corridor had an air of quiet luxury.

Mistress Delice pushed open one half of a set of double doors and peered into the room beyond. 'Looks like we're the last to arrive. Simone and Adele are already waiting for us. Follow me.'

The two chained women did as they were told, stepping into what, to Jessica's eyes, resembled nothing more than the backstage area of a theatre. Heavy curtains shielded this part of the room from what lay beyond, but from behind them she could hear raised male voices, and booming laughter. An expectant audience, waiting for the show to begin.

She recognised one of the women who already stood stage left as the blonde who'd been on the plane with her, but the tall redhead by her side was a stranger. Both, however, wore the same white robes and shackles that marked them out as auction lots.

'So, the last of our slaves has arrived.' Jessica recognised Damon Barada's voice, but she didn't turn her head in his direction. She suspected that wasn't how she was expected to behave, if the bowed heads and downcast eyes of the other women were any indication.

'Ladies,' he continued, 'I'm sure most of you know how this works, but for the benefit of our newcomer, Jessica, I'll explain. I am the auctioneer tonight, and you will follow my instructions at all times. Any man in the room is allowed to bid for you, except for your own husband, and once the bids have been concluded, you will become the property of the winning bidder until the end of your stay here. Is that clear?'

'Yes, sir.' Jessica didn't know where the honorific had come from, only that it seemed the appropriate form of address, even for a man who'd treated her as an equal on their previous meeting. Here, in this fantasy fiefdom, there was no equality; Damon Barada was her superior, and expected to be acknowledged as such.

'Good, then let the fun begin.' He clapped his hands, and the curtains were parted. Jessica found herself looking out on to a large room with half a dozen tables towards the back, all bearing the remnants of a recently finished meal, with half-empty wine bottles and coffee cups in evidence. Beyond those tables stood a fully stocked bar, overseen by a barman with dark, slicked-back hair, wearing a harlequin-patterned waistcoat and black bow tie. But these were minor details her eyes chose to focus on, so as not to look at the expectant group of figures who waited close to the stage. Max she recognised, along with the men who'd been their travelling companions from Antigua. The others were strangers to her. But they were all clearly here for one purpose – to bid on the lots in this outlandish auction.

'Gentlemen.' Damon addressed his audience in avuncular tones. 'I do hope you enjoyed your meal, and that you're ready for this evening's entertainment. Tonight, I am pleased to offer four slaves, each of whom is in need of training. Those of you who've been here before may well recognise the first lot – a serial offender whose misdeeds are too numerous to mention ...'

As he went into his spiel, Mistress Delice began to guide Honey to the front of the stage. As she was manoeuvred away from the rest of the group, Honey turned and gave Jessica a quick wink, as if to let her know everything would be all right. Her action earned her a sharp slap to the face from the dominatrix, Honey's shuddering response carrying more pleasure than pain.

'See how difficult the bitch is to control,' Damon said. 'Who out there thinks he's master enough to bring this one to heel?'

Hands were raised, and three or four voices rang out – Jessica found it hard to distinguish between them, though she was certain Max wasn't among those bidding to own her friend. Her heart thudded in her chest as she tried to shut out the thought that she might be the next up on the block.

'Who wants to get a better look at the slut's tits, and her luscious, round arse?' Damon asked. With a flourish, he pulled the robe from Honey's shoulders, baring her entirely, and drawing whoops and cheers from the watching men as he slipped a hand down between Honey's legs, then pulled it away to reveal how his fingers glistened with the woman's juices. 'See how wet she is. She loves this treatment!' he crowed.

To Jessica's mind, there could hardly be anything more shameful than being treated like goods for sale in front of a baying crowd, but Damon was right. When he ordered Honey to turn round so her back was to the audience and bend from the waist, which she did, rather awkwardly given her shackled state, the men's reaction showed they were looking at a willingly displayed and very wet pussy. If Jessica was forced to do the same, how would she react? Her cheeks flamed as she realised that, mortifying as the exposure would be, those men – Max included – would be able to see the indecently dewy state of her own plumped-up and gently pulsing sex.

Damon banged his hand down on the wooden lectern he stood by. 'Sold, to Rafael Dos Santos for 200 dollars! Come up and claim your slave, Rafael.'

A huge bear of a man with wildly curly hair and a goatee beard lumbered up to the stage, and handed over a number of banknotes of a design Jessica didn't recognise. Honey's leg cuffs were unfastened, but those securing her wrists to her collar remained in place as her new owner led her away.

Jessica's fears that she might be the next on the block evaporated as Damon called for Simone, and the redhead was led forward. Much as with Honey, the bidding for this slave was swift and intense, her price rising as Damon outlined just how hard Simone needed to be whipped to keep her in line.

When Simone had been claimed by her new owner – a bespectacled, studious-looking black man who'd been part of the group travelling to the island from Antigua – Damon called for Adele to step up to the block. Jessica was unable to pay any attention as he outlined the blonde's virtues as a potential slave, before stripping and displaying her just as he'd done with the other two. All she could do was stand and wonder who among the men might choose to bid for her, Jessica, once they'd heard she had no experience as a slave and was here because Max had decided she needed to be tamed.

'Move, slut,' Mistress Delice growled in her ear, and she was being pushed forward into the spotlight, too ashamed to raise her face to meet the audience's gaze as Damon Barada set the opening bid for her services at 50 dollars.

Chapter Six

Until the last of the women came on stage, Jason had been watching the auction with a detached eye. Even after everything he'd been told about Isla Barada – all the stories of dominant men using willing women as their slaves, stories that had his cock rigid in his underwear whenever he thought about them – he'd found it hard to believe that was what he would encounter when he arrived. It hadn't taken him long to discover every word was true, and more. So the thought of an auction, where all the women who'd been brought here this week by their masters were to be sold off to the highest bidder, should have had him salivating with anticipation.

However, when they'd brought the first of the slaves to the auction block, half-naked and shackled, he had remained curiously unmoved. Honey, the half-Thai girl, might have had a luscious, full-breasted body and kept her eyes suitably downcast as Damon Barada, revelling in his role as auctioneer, demonstrated all her finer points. But the vibes she gave off told Jason – and, he assumed, all the other would-be bidders – that she wasn't in the least ashamed at having the thin white robe that was the only garment she wore stripped right off her, so her bare tits and shaved pussy could be fondled and discussed in the crudest of terms. Everything about her screamed brat, and he'd never seen the appeal in a girl who deliberately acted up in order to earn herself a spanking.

As the price for Honey continued to rise – bids being made in the currency Barada jokingly called "Damon dollars", the bills he'd had designed especially for use in the resort – Jason stood back and watched the covetous expressions on the faces of the three self-made millionaires fighting to buy her. He could almost smell the testosterone, coming off them in waves, as each attempted to outbid the others. Not for the first time since he'd arrived, he felt out of his depth among the company in which he'd found himself.

No doubt Harry Lieberman had thought he'd been doing the right thing by treating Jason to this trip. And it was far from the first present he'd been bought by a celebrity client grateful for the amount of weight his training regime had helped them shed, or the way he'd helped them to bulk up their body in preparation for a role in a demanding action film. Usually, though, he received a nice watch or a crate of champagne to say thank you, nothing as unorthodox as Lieberman's gift.

But then, he considered, nothing about the newspaper magnate was orthodox. They'd learnt a lot about each other in the two months it had taken Lieberman to shed 25 pounds and fit once more in the suit he'd worn for his marriage to his third wife. However, it was only towards the end of their time together that Harry had confessed he'd taken Jason on as his personal trainer having been given his details from a friend who was a regular at Club

Martinet. Until then, Jason hadn't even considered the possibility that his client might be a fellow scene player. Having established their mutual interest in BDSM, he'd expected Lieberman to conform to the cliché of the high-powered businessman who craved nothing more than to give up all responsibility and be thrashed for his misdeeds by a skilled dominatrix. Instead, he turned out to be as dominant as Jason, never happier than when he had some sweet, submissive beauty grovelling at his feet, though he confined his play to private parties where he didn't run the risk of being recognised by members of the public. 'I might own a couple of scandal sheets,' he'd commented dryly, 'but that doesn't mean I want to be exposed in any of them.'

That's when he'd first brought up the subject of Isla Barada. 'You'd love it there, Jason,' he'd said.

'I'm sure I would. If I could afford it,' Jason had replied, only half-joking.

Now here he was, courtesy of Harry Lieberman's generosity. He must remember to thank the man when he got back to London; after all, it wasn't Harry's fault that none of the slaves on display tonight appealed to Jason's personal tastes.

After bratty Honey had come Simone, tall even in her bare feet, her russet hair long enough to cover her breasts when her scant covering was stripped from her. From the graphic description of Simone's various misdemeanours and the severity of the punishment she would require for each of them, Jason rapidly established that Simone was a pain slut. Again, most of the other masters in the crowd would no doubt view that as a virtue, but Jason enjoyed the psychological aspect of domination as much as, if not more than, the physical. He liked to break a woman with his words, as well as his whip, and he couldn't see Simone responding to that kind of treatment.

As for Adele, the third slave to step up to the block, she was just too young for him. Barely into her 20s, she was the archetypal trophy wife. With her collagen-augmented pout and improbably big, round breasts, she reminded him of Chelsee King, the reality TV star whose fitness DVD he'd worked on earlier in the year. If it had been the whiny, self-absorbed Chelsee they'd placed up on the stage, inviting someone to claim her so they could spank some sense into her pampered arse, Jason would have been first in the queue. The thought of ordering her lookalike to do whatever took his fancy, whether that was licking his boots clean or sucking his cock, held a certain appeal, but if he was honest with himself, what he really wanted was the chance to indulge his fantasies of dominating a gorgeous MILF.

Almost as if someone had read his mind, Damon Barada announced, 'Gentlemen, may I present the final lot of the night – Max Sheringham's slut of a wife, Jessica,' and a blonde in her early 40s, wearing the same thin robe as all the other slaves, had been half-dragged on to the stage.

She wasn't feigning her reluctance to be auctioned, or her shame at being bared for her audience as the robe was pulled off her to reveal her mature body. Unlike the other wives on display tonight, Jessica was a novice, being paraded and sold for the first time; he recognised that instinctively, and something deep inside him responded to the knowledge. His cock stirred, hardening at the sight of Jessica, cruelly exposed and unable to shield her breasts or her pussy with her hands bound behind her back. She could barely look at the crowd from behind her hair, and he could only begin to imagine the thoughts that might be running through her mind. He wanted her, wanted to bend her to his will and teach her what it meant to submit, and he would do whatever it took to make that happen.

Or so he thought. When Damon Barada asked who was prepared to start the bidding at 50 dollars, he spoke up confidently enough.

'Sixty!' came the response from the other side of the room. The German accent gave his rival bidder away, and hardened Jason's resolve to win this auction.

He'd overheard Sebastian Voller on his first evening here, complaining loudly about Barada's insistence that dominants should supply their sub with a safeword – the only hard and fast rule on this fantasy island, apart from the stipulation that all men wear a condom when fucking a woman who wasn't their own long-term bed partner. 'I don't believe in safewords,' Voller had muttered, the manner in which he almost spat out the word reinforcing his contempt for the concept. 'A slave may say they have a limit, but they can all be pushed further than any of them thinks they are prepared to go.'

Jason hadn't responded; he'd met men like Voller before. Men who seemed in perpetual danger of crossing the line from dominance into full-blown sadism. An experienced submissive like Honey or Simone would probably be able to handle his excessive demands, but this man could very easily destroy Jessica Sheringham without meaning to. He couldn't allow that to happen.

He raised his voice, making sure Barada heard him.

'Seventy dollars!'

The bids rose, Jason and Sebastian battling for Jessica between them. None of the other three women had been sold for more than 200 dollars – money which went to Damon's personal charity, the Barada Foundation, which helped those who had been victims of natural disasters – but almost before Jason realised it, Jessica's price was hovering close to the 500 dollar mark, pretty much the limit of what he could afford. He'd have to drop out, but that would let Voller win.

'Do I hear 500?' Barada enquired, looking in Jason's direction.

Jason was about to shake his head, conceding the auction and resigning himself to five days of relying on the resort's house girls for his pleasure, until he heard a voice in his ear. 'Say yes.'

Glancing to his side, he found himself looking into Max Sheringham's intense dark gaze. 'But I can't –'

'Don't worry, I'll stand you the money. Just keep bidding. There's no way I'm letting that bastard get his hands on my wife.'

Jason didn't argue, curious as he was to learn what had caused Sheringham's obvious dislike of the German. Instead, he piped up, 'Five hundred dollars.'

Voller, who'd no doubt been expecting Jason to walk away long before now, swallowed down his surprise and kept on bidding. Only when the price reached 860 dollars did he finally spit, 'I'm out. The bitch isn't worth half that – but you'll find that out soon enough.' With that, he stalked over to the bar, casting sour glances at Jason over his shoulder as he went.

'Congratulations, Mr Raynes,' Barada said as Jason

approached the stage, clutching the fistful of Damon dollars Max had slipped him to pay Jessica's auction price. 'You have yourself a slave.'

'Thank you.' He handed over the money, silently thanking Max Sheringham for his generosity. A leash was clipped into the D-ring at the front of Jessica's collar, the other end being pressed into Jason's hand. Mistress Delice handed him the keys to Jessica's wrist cuffs, which he slipped into his trouser pocket.

Awkwardness overtook him. The fantasy of buying a slave, of commanding her to do whatever he wished, of leading her around naked and compliant, was one thing; the reality something else altogether. He'd played out scenes in Club Martinet where he'd been firmly in charge, but always with someone he'd made some kind of connection to beforehand. This, he had to remind himself, was a complete stranger. They'd never as much as said hello to each other before this moment. More than that, she appeared to have almost no experience of acting as a submissive, if Damon's description of her was to be believed. For all Max's insistence that he keep bidding till he won the auction, he couldn't help wondering if he'd done the right thing.

Aware of Damon's amused gaze on him, he tugged at the leash. 'Come with me,' he ordered Jessica, the words coming out more gruffly than he'd intended.

She didn't disobey, didn't dig in her heels and ask where he thought he was taking her, as bratty Honey might have. He led her over to the bar, making sure to stand well away from Voller, who was nursing a glass of what appeared to be whiskey and muttering to another of the failed bidders about the auction being a joke.

Retrieving the keys to Jessica's cuffs from his pocket, he freed her hands. Her obvious relief was short lived when he caught hold of her wrists, and expertly fastened them together again, in front of her body this time.

He pulled his wallet out of his back pocket and found a couple of dollar bills. 'I want you to get me a beer.' He waited for her to take the money from his fingers. When she didn't, he fixed her with a stern glare. 'Right away, Jessica.'

'But, master –' The word sounded so sweet on her lips that his cock gave an involuntary lurch. 'My hands are bound.'

Inexperienced as she was, he had no intention of giving her any leeway. She was going to struggle with the task, but that only added to his sense of anticipation. 'Which means you'll have to be extra careful not to spill a drop, doesn't it? Now, get me that beer.'

Any further objection seemed to die in her throat as he gestured at her to get a move on. Clutching his money awkwardly, she managed to attract the attention of the barman and place her order. Jason couldn't help but notice that the guy's eyes were firmly glued to Jessica's bare breasts as he poured the beer. He couldn't blame him; his own thoughts were of taking her pebbled nipples between his lips and sucking till her mouth opened in a soft O of need.

The barman put the beer glass down on the counter and plucked the money from Jessica's fingers. On tiptoes, she reached up to grasp the glass in both hands and brought it back to Jason. Even though she took tiny, careful steps, her whole concentration fixed on trying not to spill the drink, the man who'd been talking to Voller took a pace back, not realising she was behind him, and nudged into her. A little of the liquid slopped over the rim, splashing the exposed skin of her rounded belly. He began to apologise to her, but quickly stopped when he caught sight of Jason and the realisation of what Jessica had been asked to do appeared to dawn on him. His expression turned to one that clearly indicated what a lucky bastard he thought Jason was.

The look of contrition on her face as Jessica handed the glass to him had Jason aching to bend her over the bar counter and slide his cock into her cunt.

'I'm so sorry, master. I tried, I really did, but –'

Jason shook his head. 'I gave you a simple task, and you didn't manage it. You know what that means, don't you?'

Before he could begin to outline what Jessica's failure might mean for her in terms of punishment, a roar went up somewhere behind them. He turned to see that the next part of the evening's entertainment was about to begin.

Chapter Seven

At first, Jessica couldn't see what was causing all the commotion. Only when her master, as she was already coming to think of him, ordered her to turn and look did she see the contraption that had been hauled into the centre of the room. A large, sturdy wooden frame, supported on a base which enabled it to be wheeled from place to place, it had thick leather cuffs, similar to the ones that still kept her hands fastened together, attached to its four corners. And those cuffs were currently buckled around the wrists and ankles of Simone, the red-haired submissive. The girl's limbs were stretched tight, splaying her out like a star, every inch of her stunning body glistening with a light sheen of sweat. The sight was terrifying, as Jessica imagined how she would look strapped to that thing, her arms and legs pulled out even more tautly, given that Simone must have a good four inches of height on her. Terrifying, and yet her pussy still pulsed with hot anticipation.

'What – what is that, master?' she asked, her voice little more than a frightened squeak.

'First of all, Jessica, you must learn that from now on you don't speak until I address you, but I'll let your indiscretion go this time. Secondly, it's a whipping frame, and a bloody impressive one at that.'

She didn't need to ask any more questions. Instead, she took another sideways look at the man who'd paid what seemed like an obscene amount of money to own her for the week, trying to decide what she made of him.

When she'd been led to the front of the stage by Mistress Delice, and Damon Barada had begun to list the reasons why she needed to be, as he'd put it, "brought to heel", she'd barely been able to raise her gaze to look at the audience. There'd been an audible murmur of appreciation when he'd pulled the robe off her shoulders, revealing her body to the crowd. Despite herself, she couldn't help thinking back to that night in Envied when her unknown partner had as good as stripped her on the dance floor, and the crazy excitement that had overtaken her. For the first time, she realised that though the men here might have all the money and status, her naked beauty and willingness to submit gave her a power of her own.

Still, she'd found herself praying she wouldn't be bought by the leathery old goat who was married to Adele; the thought of his age-spotted hands pawing her sent a shudder of distaste through her. So it was with some relief that the bidding had been conducted between two of the youngest men in the room. The pretty boy with the German accent, Sebastian whatever his name was – he was definitely her type, with his shoulder-length blond hair, pouting mouth and long, lean body. Having to obey his commands wouldn't be all bad. But it was the other man who seemed the more determined to secure her services, and if she were honest, she wouldn't have looked at him twice in the street. When Honey had described a couple of the men staying here as "hot", she just couldn't have had this one in mind. Considerably taller than Max, dark stubble bristled on his chin, and his jawline was too heavy, his nose too big for Jessica to consider him as anything but a piece of rough. More than that, something about him didn't quite fit with the other men in the room; he didn't seem to share their ease in these opulent surroundings, their belief that they were entitled to be treated with constant deference. From nowhere, the phrase had popped into her head: pauper masquerading as a prince. Could he be a member of Barada's staff, inflating her price so the other man would be forced to pay more? Yet he'd had no problem producing the money when the German dropped out of the bidding, and he'd led her away with a wide grin of satisfaction on his face.

Now, as she stared in fear and guilty eagerness at Simone, suspended in the whipping frame and awaiting whatever punishment was to come, she felt her master – Jason, hadn't Barada called him? – run a caressing hand down the length of her back and onto her bum cheek. His fingers weren't calloused, as she'd expect of someone who did manual work for a living, but neither did he have soft hands like Max. Why, she wondered, was it so important for her to learn anything about him? She'd never bothered getting to know the men she hooked up with in Envied, or the other clubs. But then she'd been the one in charge on those occasions, taking what she wanted from them before returning home to her husband. It didn't matter who they were, what thoughts and needs they had. This was different.

Her master gave her bottom a gentle slap, just hard

enough to attract her attention. 'It's about to begin, Jessica. Watch carefully. Ask questions if you feel the need. It's important that you learn from this.'

'Yes, master.' She couldn't help wondering exactly what he expected her to learn from this perverse exhibition. Though one thing still nagged at her. 'Master, why is she being punished? I don't remember her doing anything wrong.'

'There could be any number of reasons. She could have said something to displease her new owner, she might have spilled a drink – just like you did – or her husband could have asked that regular whippings be part of her treatment while she's here. I reckon it's the last of those. Everything Barada said about Simone when he was auctioning her off tells me she's a full-on pain slut.'

Every answer begged a dozen more. What the hell was a pain slut? How much say did a woman's husband have in how she was disciplined? Was Jason seriously thinking of strapping her to that same frame because she hadn't brought his beer to him without spilling some?

The man who'd bought Simone approached the frame, distracting Jessica from her ever more anxious musings. He carried a small whip with a dozen or so tails, all about a foot long, which he trailed though his fingers. The leather thongs, dyed a vivid shade of purple, contrasted arrestingly with his dark skin, and Jessica couldn't help feeling she was watching a piece of theatre, as much as a punishment. The thought prompted another question.

'Master,' she whispered, aware that speaking too loudly would break the reverent hush that had descended on the room. 'Why does Simone's new owner look so familiar? Is he an actor?'

Jason shook his head. 'That's Wesley Cole. You know, the man behind *Furious Frogs*?'

She didn't own the game herself, but Jessica knew enough people who were addicted to playing it on their phones and tablet computers. And every newspaper story detailing the astonishing amounts of money the game's creator had earned was accompanied, she now recalled, by a photo of the man who was about to thrash the helpless Simone.

Cole held the whip up to Simone's face, letting her take a good look at the implement he was about to use on her.

'Looks like he's going easy on her, using that flogger,' Jason informed Jessica, guiding her away from the bar to join the ring of spectators gathered round the whipping frame. 'At dinner last night, Chester Macken said when they're in their playroom at home, he likes to use a bullwhip on Simone. Mind you, it takes quite a bit of skill to handle one of those without causing serious damage.'

Starting at Simone's shoulders, Cole softly dragged the broad leather tails across her bare skin. As they brushed her nipples, already hard and standing out from the pale pink haloes surrounding them, the redhead gave a moan. Everything about her demeanour suggested she wanted this, craved the punishment. The whip continued on its teasing trail, down over her stomach to slip between her legs. Simone's moans deepened, which was the moment when Cole pulled the instrument away.

'Silence,' he ordered Simone. It was the only thing he said before moving to stand behind her and bringing the flogger down for the first time. The tails struck the girl's flesh, landing in quick succession on her arse. She hissed between her teeth, but made no other sound.

Cole flicked his wrist, lashing out again and again, striping first one buttock, then the next. Between strokes, he caressed the whip, dragging it across his palm, before bringing it down once more. The only sounds in the room were the slapping of leather on skin and the low murmuring of male voices as the audience discussed between themselves how well the girl was taking her whipping.

The skin of Simone's rump was taking on a mottled, pinkish hue as Cole continued to beat it, but if the blows were causing her any pain, she gave no real indication apart from an occasional hiccupping whimper.

Cole changed tack. Now the flogger landed on the tops of her thighs, just below the crease where they met Simone's bum cheeks. The slave grunted and writhed in her bonds, but to Jessica the motions looked more like those of a woman in thrall to pleasure, rather than one who was trying to escape the stinging blows.

Across the room, Jessica noticed Max, standing at the edge of crowd with a brandy snifter clutched in his fist. All his focus seemed to be on the kinky tableau before him, as Cole stalked round to the other side of the frame. Now Jessica saw the real genius of this form of restraint: it left the slave exposed to punishment, front and back, with no need for the dominant to break off from the whipping to reposition her.

'Master, he's not going to hit her there, is he?' Jessica asked anxiously, as Cole brushed the whip over Simone's visibly quivering stomach.

'Oh yes,' Jason assured her, the throaty catch in his voice telling her how much the prospect turned him on. Jessica's gaze flickered downwards, to the crotch of his dark trousers. The fabric was noticeably stretched around the solid bulk of his cock. 'And I doubt he'll draw the line at whipping her belly.'

The little whip slashed down again, landing on the soft swell of Simone's stomach and making her moan. He gave her half a dozen swift strokes there, reddening the pale flesh, then paused, clutching the ends of the flogger's tails in his fist.

'I can see you've had nowhere near enough yet, slut,' Cole commented, 'and I've no intention of stopping until I hear you beg for mercy. Maybe this will do the trick …'

With that, he flicked out the whip in the direction of her breasts, hitting them with an audible slap. Unable to quite believe what she'd just seen, Jessica tried not to let her mouth fall open in horror. If her hands hadn't been cuffed, she'd have reached up to cradle her own tits in sympathy. But though Simone cried out, she didn't ask her tormentor to end the punishment. Another blow struck her breasts, and another. Angry red marks marred their creamy perfection, and the fat buds of her nipples jutted out further, almost inviting Cole to whip them again.

Instead, he brought the flogger sharply up between Simone's legs, slapping her there. Groans of admiration and lust issued from the watching men as Cole showed them the tails of the whip, glistening wet with Simone's pussy juices. Jessica moaned, trying to imagine how much it must hurt to have that wicked little whip strike such a sensitive, intimate area. Cole repeated the action and Simone yelled again, jerking and humping the air in a frenzy. Though she must have been in pain, the noises she made were all too obviously those of a woman in the throes of orgasm.

'She – she's coming,' Jessica murmured.

'I told you, she's a pain slut,' Jason replied. 'Some submissives get off on the psychological side of being dominated, but for ones like Simone, it's all about the physical. Pain mixes with pleasure till they don't know where one ends and the other one starts, and that's the result.'

At last, Simone's spasms of pleasure died away, and she hung limp in her bonds. Cole raised his flogging arm again, about to resume the punishment, only for the girl to sob, 'Please, master, no more. I beg you to stop.'

'Very good,' Cole replied, dropping the flogger to the floor and beginning to release Simone from the cuffs that held her in place.

'She could have taken more,' Jason declared, 'but I reckon she wants him to take her away and deal with her properly, in private.'

'So what happens now, master?' Jessica asked, as Jason drained the rest of his beer. Visions flashed through her head of him strapping her into the whipping frame, and forcing her to undergo the same kind of public punishment that had been meted out to Simone. She looked over to where Max had been standing, wondering whether he'd come to her aid if this man tried to force her into taking a flogging she didn't feel ready to receive, but, like most of the other male guests, he'd wandered away once the scene had finished.

'Now,' Jason told her, setting down his empty glass on the bar counter, 'we go to my room and get to know each other a little better.'

Taking hold of the leash that hung down between her breasts, Jason led Jessica out of the ballroom. She took one last look behind her, but Max was nowhere to be seen. He'd abandoned her to a virtual stranger, and she had no idea when she might be reunited with him again, or what might happen to her before she was.

Chapter Eight

Jason Raynes had a suite on the first floor of the main resort building, up a wide, carpeted staircase from the reception area. She followed him along the corridor, still not entirely comfortable with being made to walk around naked in the company of a fully dressed man, but realising she no longer had anything to hide from all the men who'd seen her displayed on the auction block.

Unlocking the door to his room, he guided Jessica inside, and switched on a free-standing lamp that filled the bedroom with a soft, golden glow. She looked around, admiring a sofa and armchair designed along clean, Scandinavian lines, and a bed that was surely big enough to sleep three people in comfort. A huge, plasma-screen TV hung on one wall, and a small glass and chrome cabinet contained what looked like a DVD player, iPod dock, and satellite receiver – all sleek, state of the art boys' toys. Clearly, Damon Barada did not believe in sparing any expense when it came to ensuring any and every need was catered to.

The big, double windows that led out onto a balcony were open; though it was too dark to see what lay beyond them, the soft pull and drag of waves on sand let Jessica know the ocean could not be too far away. Quiet luxury, just what she'd expected when Max had told her about Isla Barada, except now she knew it existed for the male guests alone.

Her master took the keys to her cuffs from his trouser pocket and released her. This time, he didn't promptly re-cuff her wrists. She eyed him warily, wondering if he might have some other cruel trick up his sleeve. After all, there was the small matter of the beer she'd spilled to be resolved. He didn't strike her as the type who would forget something like that.

He glanced at his watch. 'Time for a quick lesson before bed, I think.'

At the mention of bed, she found herself trying to stifle a yawn. Even taking into account the afternoon nap she'd shared with Honey, it had still been an awfully long day, and she needed her sleep. Max always complained about how tetchy she became if she didn't get a solid eight hours.

'Now, now, Jessica,' Jason reprimanded her. 'Your husband expects me to return a properly trained slave to him, and I don't have a great deal of time to do it. But the sooner you get this right, the sooner you get to sleep.'

'Yes, master.' She knew she sounded sulky, but she didn't care. She wanted Max, wanted the comfort of her own bed, and knew she wasn't likely to get either of those things for a while.

'Right, the first thing any good submissive needs to know is how to get into the display position. I want you to kneel on the floor, resting your bottom on your heels.' When Jessica didn't immediately rush to obey, Jason snapped, 'Kneel. You're only racking up the demerit marks by stringing this out, and the more of those you earn this week, the harsher your punishment will be.'

Mention of punishment sent Jessica dropping to her knees, anxious not to displease her master further.

'Good,' he said. 'Now, spread your thighs nice and wide. Show me that little pink pussy of yours.'

Revealing herself to him in that fashion would be yet another of the many humiliations she'd been forced to endure today, yet her traitorous pussy leaked its thick nectar at the thought. Unable to meet his gaze, she parted her legs and let him admire the wet folds of her sex lips and the nub of her clit, nestling at their apex.

'What a gorgeous cunt you have,' he told her, taking a good, long look. 'Just made to be licked and fucked and displayed to your master. But you're not quite in full position yet. Put your hands behind your head and link your fingers together.'

She did as he asked, aware that the movement raised her breasts and thrust them out towards him. From the grin that crossed his stubbled face, he appreciated the effect.

'Now, every time I give you the command "Display", that's how I want you to present yourself. It doesn't matter where we are, or who we're with. Do you understand?'

'Yes, master.' She half-hoped he wouldn't force her to display herself to other men, half-hoped he would. If that was her lesson for the evening, she thought, she'd learnt it quickly. Maybe he'd let her sleep now.

When he reached into one of the drawers of his nightstand, she realised he had other ideas. He withdrew a vibrator, still in its plastic packaging. Tearing it open and slotting a couple of batteries into its chamber, he brought it over to her.

'D'you know what would really please me?' he asked. 'If you used this on yourself.'

The toy was of black latex, thickly veined, looking very similar to the one Mistress Delice, in her guise as a customs officer, had pulled from Jessica's luggage.

'Damon's very generous,' Jason commented. 'He equips all the suites with a selection of toys for us to use. Of course, some people like to bring their own, like Wesley Cole and that tasty custom-made flogger of his. But for what I have in mind, this is just perfect.'

He held out the vibrator. Jessica obediently unlinked her fingers, noticing they trembled slightly as she took it from him. She should be protesting, telling him she couldn't do this. Just like she should have protested more strongly when Max had made her seduce Darragh on the plane, or when she'd been ordered to strip and spread her legs for inspection in the interrogation suite. But each time, she'd done what had been asked of her willingly, the submissive streak she'd never realised lay so deeply within her responding to these ever more outrageous requests.

'Do it, Jessica. Make yourself come for me.'

Turning the base of the toy, she felt it buzz beneath her fingers, its vibrations strong and steady. After everything that had been done to Simone, this wasn't so bad, she considered. It wasn't like she hadn't used one of her own vibrators to put on a show for Max, back in the days before their sex life had taken a back seat to the pressures of his business.

Jason's gaze was fixed on her pussy as she pressed

the tip of the vibe into her slippery cleft. The vibrations were too strong, the intensity on her sensitive flesh too much, and she dialled them down a notch or two. She sensed he wouldn't want her to come too soon, before he'd really had a chance to enjoy the performance she was about to put on for him.

Jessica ran the vibrator up and down her slit, almost amused at the avid way Jason's eyes followed its progress, like a greyhound chasing a hare. Assured of his total attention, she pushed the rounded head into her channel, just a little way, feeling herself spread around its thickness. A plastic cock like this could never match the real thing, but right now it gave her exactly the stimulation she needed. Its constant vibrations pulsed through her, making her pussy walls twitch and causing a similar response in her rear passage. She recalled the sensation of Darragh's thick shaft reaming her arse, and thought of slipping the toy into herself there, then dismissed the idea. One glance at the crotch of her master's trousers, tented out by the force of his erection, told her how much he was enjoying the sight of that fake dick slipping in and out of her hole – and this was about pleasing him, after all.

With the vibrator lodged deep inside herself, she put a finger to her clit, knowing it wouldn't take much of that additional stimulation to make her come. Her nipples were taut crests, and she reached up to pinch one, mewling as fierce sensation darted down to her sex. She threw her head back as her pleasure mounted, exposing the pale length of her throat to Jason in a gesture of submission and abandon.

'Are you close, Jessica?' he asked.

'Yes, master,' she replied, voice husky with need.

'Then you have ten seconds. If you don't come within that time, you don't come at all.'

How could he ask her to come on cue? It was cruel, unnatural. Yet, as his voice counted down the seconds, she felt herself peaking, every muscle tense and tight as the relentless vibrations become too much to resist.

'Four ... Three ... Two ...'

'Ah! I – I'm ...' Jessica's words faded into garbled moans, as her muscles convulsed around the plastic cock and she orgasmed under Jason's unblinking gaze. She slumped back on her heels, the vibrator, still buzzing, slipping from her fingers to the floor.

Jason picked it up and switched it off, then came to crouch beside her. 'Good girl,' he murmured.

Those two simple words of praise woke something in her. Where before he had been stern and commanding, now his tone was tender. She'd followed his instructions and she'd pleased him, just as he'd asked her to. Looking up into his face, she noticed for the first time that his eyes were the brightest cornflower blue, and they were smiling at her. Something melted inside her, as she experienced for the first time the real satisfaction that came from doing as she'd been told. All the harsh words, all the humiliation, had been worth it for this moment.

'Time for bed,' he told her, reaching out to help her to her feet.

'But, master ...' She felt shy of asking the question, even though she knew his cock must still be rock hard. He hadn't as much as stroked himself while he'd been watching her, and she marvelled at his iron willpower. 'Wouldn't you like me to do anything for you?' The implication in her words was obvious. Her mouth was his if he wanted it, her pussy too. Whatever he needed to relieve his pent-up desire.

He shook his head. 'Later. Now go in the bathroom and clean yourself up. And this –' He handed her the vibrator, sticky with her juices.

Jessica went into the bathroom, to discover it was larger than the room she shared with Honey. And what might be happening to Honey now? With a guilty start, Jessica realised this was the first time she'd thought of her friend since she had been led away by her new master, Dos Santos. Perhaps she was in their room even now, waiting for Jessica to arrive so she could share the details of her evening's adventure.

But when Jessica emerged from the bathroom, having washed both herself and the vibrator with a vanilla-scented body wash that, like so much else in this suite, had been provided for the guests' use, it quickly became clear that Jason didn't intend her to return to her own room tonight.

While she'd been out of the room, he'd stripped down to nothing but a pair of black jersey trunks that clung to the substantial outline of his cock and balls. Whatever he did for a living, he must spend a lot of spare time in the gym; the muscles of his stomach were clearly defined, giving him the kind of six-pack she'd only ever seen on the models in adverts for expensive cologne, and when he turned away to place his watch on the nightstand, she almost whistled in appreciation at the firmness of his arse, her inner cougar briefly reasserting itself.

Slipping under the bedcovers, Jason beckoned her to join him, but when she turned aside the sheet on the other side of the bed to his, he snapped, 'What do you think you're doing? Your place is at the bottom of the bed.' When she followed the direction of his pointing finger, she saw that he'd already laid out a throw, decorated with a pattern of palm leaves, for her to sleep under. How foolish of her to imagine they might have slept side by side, like she would have with Max. In her world, the bottom of the bed was where a family pet would sleep. Could that really be how her master viewed her?

She climbed on to the bed, and pulled the throw over herself.

'Oh, and one last thing. Just in case you have any bright ideas about trying to sneak out of here as soon as I fall asleep …'

He got out of bed, and bent to retrieve something from the floor beneath it. Horrified, Jessica realised he was holding a length of chain with a cuff at one end. Glancing down, she saw that the other end of the chain was securely fixed to the bed leg. Her master wrapped the restraint around her ankle, fastening it tight. Unlike the ones she'd worn earlier, this cuff had a little padlock attached; once he'd snapped it shut, Jessica knew she wasn't getting free until he decided.

With a little grunt of satisfaction, he climbed back under the covers and switched off the lamp.

Oh Max, she thought, curling up in a miserable ball. How could you have done this to me?

Chapter Nine

He lay awake for a long time after he'd turned out the light, listening to the soft breathing of the woman who slept at the foot of his bed. It had taken a considerable effort of will not to order her to suck him off after she'd made herself come so beautifully with that big, black vibrator, and his cock was still a rigid bar in his underwear. And she'd have let him thrust it all the way to the back of her throat – her desire to please him had been written all over her face. What had he been trying to prove by not fucking her mouth? Whatever, it had backfired on him; she was sleeping like a baby while he lay staring up at the ceiling, listening to the gentle murmur of the ocean, unable to drift off.

Eventually, he clambered out of bed, careful not to wake her, and padded to the bathroom. Only one thing would help him sleep now. Pulling his cock free of his underwear, he gripped it at its root, already feeling excitement churning in his belly. As he ran his fingers up and down the swollen shaft, he watched himself in the mirror. This should be Jessica, easing the velvet sheath of skin back and forth, cradling his aching balls in her palm; Jessica bringing him to an orgasm that threatened to shatter his sanity. Wanking with ever more ferocious strokes, he thought of all the things he would order her to do before the week was out, all the ways he would find to bring that endearing flush of shame to her soft cheeks. He would make her battle against his demands, relishing the flash of spirit that had driven Max Sheringham to bring her here for training, knowing that ultimately she would surrender to him. He pictured her lips wrapped around his cock, her pussy and arse yielding to him as he fucked her. He could still hear the noises she'd made as she came, the depth of her passion impossible to ignore; see those puffy pink cunt lips stretched around the vibrator's thick, black shaft. Next time she fucked herself with that toy, he'd instruct her to lick it clean of her juices afterwards.

That was the image that pushed him over the edge, biting the fleshy pad of his thumb to muffle his groans and avoid waking her. His spunk jetted out, splashing into the toilet bowl. When he glanced at his reflection again, the colour in his cheeks was high, his eyes feverishly bright, but his frustrations had eased and he knew he'd be able to sleep now.

Tiredness was already overcoming him as he walked back to the bed. He slid under the covers once more. Jessica, no doubt lost in her own dreams of the day just gone, didn't even stir.

His normal routine involved waking early and going for a run before breakfast. Even here, where time seemed to have its own slow rhythm and guests were actively encouraged to do as little as possible, he'd been keeping to his usual habits, jogging a couple of miles or so along the beach while everyone else slept, feeling the sense of wellbeing that came from regular exercise.

This morning, he didn't wake till one of the house girls bustled into the bedroom, bringing him his breakfast on a tray.

'Good morning, sir.' She beamed at him, pulling a table over to the side of the bed and setting the tray down on it. Her glance settled on Jessica, who'd been roused by the sound of voices and crockery rattling, and was even now struggling to sit up while using the throw to preserve something of her modesty. 'Can I get anything for her?'

Jason considered the question for a moment. Jessica looked adorable, her hair mussed and her limbs heavy with sleep. He took a perverse delight in replying to the maid's query in kind, talking about his submissive as though she wasn't even worthy of being referred to by name.

'Bring whatever has been decided on for her breakfast. And we'll be going down to the beach, so find her something suitable to wear. I'll leave it to your discretion.'

'Yes, sir.' The girl's face dimpled prettily. In his everyday life, Jason wasn't used to women routinely treating him as though he was the centre of the universe, and he still found it a little odd how his every wish was deferred to. Still, he determined to make the most of it; he'd be back in his old routine soon enough.

Breakfast consisted of a bowl of granola, packed with nuts and dried cranberries, and topped with yoghurt, washed down with freshly squeezed orange juice, and a cafetière of coffee. If he'd wanted, he could have had croissants and honey, scrambled eggs on rye toast or even a fry-up – nothing appeared to be too much trouble for the kitchen staff. Jason sipped his juice and regarded Jessica. Her expression was troubled, and her fingers clutched and released the edge of the throw.

'Do you wish to ask me something?' he said, remembering that last night he'd told her only to speak after being given permission.

'Please, master, I – I need to use the bathroom.' She sounded embarrassed to have to make the request. 'Rather urgently.' He was about to send her on her way, until she adjusted her position, rising to her knees, and he noticed the chain that still kept her tethered to the bed.

'Very well.' He set down his glass, and fished the padlock key from among the clutter on his nightstand. Once he'd released her, he said, 'Right, off you go, and be quick about it. And leave the bathroom door open so I can see you.'

'But, master …'

'Are you daring to question an order?'

She lowered her eyes. 'No, master.'

'Well, do as I say before I change my mind.' Jessica didn't need to know that he had no intention of peering into the bathroom, but presenting her with the possibility that he'd be watching her perform such a private act would add to her humiliation.

By the time she'd finished her ablutions, the maid had returned with Jessica's breakfast – a bowl of yoghurt and tropical fruit – which she set down on the floor, close to Jason's side of the bed. She also carried a pair of flat, cork-soled sandals and a scrap of leopard-print fabric masquerading as a swimsuit.

'Once you've eaten,' Jason informed Jessica, 'you're to dress and ready yourself for the beach.'

She glanced at the bowl on the floor, then at Jason. 'But, master, there's no spoon. You don't seriously expect me to –?'

He cut her plea off abruptly. 'Of course I do. And if you continue to be such a big baby about things, I'll keep the maid here to watch you eat. Would you like that?'

'No, master.'

As Jason waved the maid away, Jessica obediently got down on all fours, and began to eat from the bowl. He settled himself comfortably against the pillows, munching on his own breakfast as he watched her efforts to lap up the mixture of creamy yoghurt and soft, ripe fruits. How delicious she looked, he thought, striving to do whatever it took to please him. She didn't need to know just yet that every time she argued, every time she objected to one of his orders, she was earning herself more in the way of punishment. Mentally, he was compiling a list of demerits, and on the night before he handed her over to Max, he would make her pay for every single one of them. For now, he was happy to admire the little, cat-like lapping motions of her tongue as she did her best to lick the bowl clean, and the way her bare breasts swayed beneath her as she moved.

Fuck, just watching her was getting him hard again. If Jessica chose to look up, she couldn't fail to notice the way his cock had made a tent of the bedsheets, advertising his need for her. He ached to sink it into her pussy, but then another idea struck him.

'I've finished, master,' Jessica said. 'Every last drop.'

She sat back on her heels, giving him a clear view of the empty bowl. Little blobs of yoghurt adorned the tip of her nose and her chin, almost begging to be kissed away.

'Not quite,' he replied, pushing the covers aside to reveal his naked body and proud, upstanding dick. Before her clearly disbelieving eyes, he took a spoonful of yoghurt from the little that remained in his own dish, and smeared it along his shaft from root to tip. 'This needs to be licked up too.'

He sat with his feet planted on the floor, legs widely spread, encouraging her to nestle between them. After only a moment's hesitation, Jessica crawled over, into the lee of his muscled thighs, and bent her head to take him between his lips. Just the feel of her wet mouth engulfing his helmet had him gripping the sheets and fighting not to come. Think about everything that's waiting for you at home, he told himself: the bills that will have arrived in your absence; the clients who'll have been neglecting their exercises and stuffing their faces with chips without you around to supervise their routine. Concentrating on those unwelcome images brought him back from the brink, so he could fully enjoy the manner in which Jessica was assiduously licking him clean.

Strands of her blonde hair fell about her face, and he caught them up in his fist, giving him a better view of her mouth working on his cock. She was the perfect picture of submission. Her lips were stretched around the thickness of him, her cheeks hollowed with the suction, and her eyes were half-closed – whether in pleasure or because she was too ashamed to meet his gaze, he didn't know. Keeping a grip of her hair enabled him to push her head a little further down onto his shaft, encouraging her to take as much of him as she could. The only sounds in the room were the soft, gobbling noises Jessica was making around his cock, his own tense, harsh breathing, and, from the distance, the rhythmic hiss of the ocean. He fought the urge to jerk his hips and fuck her face properly.

When he pulled her off his dick, he could see a distinct line, like a high water mark, indicating how much of his length she'd managed to clean. 'Finish it,' he ordered, and she set to lapping up the rest of the yoghurt from the base of his cock. Some of it had dribbled down over his balls and into the crack of his butt, and she cleaned up the creamy trails without complaint. Jason groaned as the point of her tongue snaked briefly into the pucker of his arsehole. He should have kept the maid here to witness the sight of this gorgeous, wilful cougar obediently licking his arse. Pleasure trembled through his body, and he knew he couldn't delay his orgasm much longer.

'I'm going to come,' he told Jessica, 'and you're going to take it all in that hot, slutty mouth of yours.'

'Yes, master,' she replied, before taking the head of his cock between her lips once more.

'Play with my balls,' he ordered her, and at once she cradled both tight orbs in her palm. The sensation of her fingers rolling them gently in their sacs while her tongue moved over his helm in rapid figures of eight was too much for him to resist. With a cry of triumph, he filled her mouth with his seed, feeling the muscles of his arse clench in time with each pumping spasm.

The strength of his orgasm left him drained, and he fell back on the bed. Jessica smiled up at him, licking the last drops of come from her lips.

'You were –' He was about to add "amazing", but somehow it didn't feel appropriate to compliment her technique, as though he was just another of her one-night stands. Pulling himself together, he said, 'You've got yoghurt on your face, girl. Go and wash it off, then get dressed.'

'Yes, master.'

As he watched her go, he thought again how unbelievably lucky he'd been to land himself such an inexperienced but obviously willing submissive. If Max Sheringham put in an appearance at the beach, he'd be sure to thank the man, and maybe give him a little sneak preview of just what he could expect when Jessica was finally returned to him. And if he wasn't there, well, Jason knew he could find some other way of making this another day to remember, both for Jessica and himself.

Chapter Ten

Jessica took a last look at her reflection in the bathroom mirror. The swimsuit that had been taken from her case for her to wear was possibly the most daring she owned, leaving very little to the imagination once it was on, and she wondered whether the maid had chosen it precisely for that reason. The halter fastening and thong bottom left most of her back and bum cheeks bare, and her nipples were visible points beneath the thin leopard-print material. She looked just what Jason had called her, hot and slutty.

Being made to suck her master's cock had turned her on more than she could have expected. Her first glimpse of that beautiful tool, every bit as long and hard as her sneaky peeks at his crotch had led her to expect, had made her pussy flood with juice. She'd really had to open her mouth wide to take him in, feeling a strange sense of achievement at managing to swallow more than half his impressive length. And though she'd never liked it when men had grabbed her hair and tried to force the pace of a blowjob to suit themselves, somehow it had seemed only right to let him take control.

What would Max say if he'd been able to see her, down on her knees, obediently licking Jason's arsehole clean of yoghurt? She couldn't help feeling he'd have approved; for some reason he seemed to get off on the thought of her being fucked by another man, as long as he knew about it. When she was finally returned to him at the end of their holiday, would she have to give him all the details? Already she'd been made to pleasure herself with the dildo while her master watched, as well as lavishing him with the best of her oral attentions. And she'd barely spent 12 hours in his company – God knew in what other ways he'd manage to degrade and humiliate her for his amusement, while simultaneously bringing her to the highest peaks of excitement.

'Come on, Jessica,' he called from the bedroom – as before, he'd made her leave the bathroom door open, allowing her no privacy. 'We haven't got all day.'

Quickly, she twisted her hair into a plait, securing it with an elasticated band from a pot of odds and ends on the bathroom counter. Satisfied with her appearance, she went to join her master. In her absence, he'd put on a pair of baggy floral shorts and a black, sleeveless T-shirt, coupling them with plastic flip-flops and aviator shades. The casual look suited him much better than the formal shirt and trousers he'd worn last night, and she wondered again exactly what he did for a living. Was he another Internet geek like Wesley Cole, happiest spending his days slouched in front of a computer screen and keeping contact with other people to a minimum? But if that was the case, how had he managed to hone those quite spectacular muscles?

Stop worrying about him, she reprimanded herself, and start worrying about what else he might have planned for you.

His eyes widened at the sight of her, but he didn't comment on her appearance. Instead, he picked up the rolled-up beach towel that lay on the bed and ordered her to follow him.

They took the back exit from the resort building, and as Jason pushed open the door, Jessica caught her first glimpse of the beach. Fine, white sand, so unspoilt she wondered whether Damon Barada employed someone to smooth it clean of footprints every night, stretched down to a crystal blue ocean. Seabirds wheeled in the air, their mournful cries carrying across the water, and the leaves of palm trees rustled in a gentle breeze. This was what she'd expected her holiday with Max to be like; long days spent lying on a sun lounger, or maybe even in a hammock stretched between trees, interspersed with a dip in the pool or a trip to the resort bar for a cooling cocktail.

Jason led the way to where a couple of towels had already been laid out on the sand. On one of them lay Honey, wearing possibly the tiniest bikini Jessica had ever seen in her life. The lime-green cups covered the big, brown discs of Honey's nipples and almost nothing else, and the bottom was a triangle of fabric so scanty it left most of her mound and sex lips bare. Having already seen her friend naked, Jessica knew every last hair on Honey's pussy had been waxed away, but any passer-by observing her as she soaked up the sun would rapidly reach the same conclusion.

Honey sat up as Jason and Jessica approached, removed her oversized sunglasses, and flashed them both a dazzling smile. She patted the towel by her side, in a clear invitation for Jessica to join her. The man who'd bought her at the auction appeared to be nowhere in sight.

Jessica went to join her, but was brought up short by Jason's barked command. 'My towel, girl.'

Of course – always the gratification of her master's needs before her own. She needed to remember that if she was to become the well-behaved submissive Max needed her to be. She unrolled the blue and green towel, with its vivid pattern of scallop seashells, and spread it out. He'd bundled up a bottle of high-factor sun lotion in the middle of the towel, and she set that aside. Jason peeled off his T-shirt; Jessica thought she heard Honey give a low, appreciative sigh at the sight of his taut stomach and broad, bare chest.

'Do you need anything else, sir?' she asked, once Jason had made himself comfortable. 'Sun lotion, perhaps? A cool drink?'

He shook his head. 'Not for the time being. I'll call you when I want you.'

With that, she was dismissed. Feeling oddly bereft, she went to lie beside Honey. Her friend giggled, prompting Jessica to prop herself up on her elbow to see what had inspired such mirth. 'See, I told you you'd be mastered by one of the hot guys.'

'You think Jason's hot? Seriously?'

'Don't you?' Honey asked. 'With those muscles and that killer smile?'

Jason didn't seem to have smiled at her that much since she'd stepped down from the auction block, she reflected – though when he had, she'd basked in the warmth of his approval. 'I don't know,' she said. 'I prefer them a little more – clean cut.'

'Well, I'd offer to trade you – I mean, I've got a master with hairy shoulders. And don't start me on all the fuzz in the crack of his arse …' Honey gave a little shudder. 'But boy, does he know how to wield a cane.' She rolled over, letting Jessica see her bottom, the perfection of its golden skin marred by three raised red lines that ran parallel to each other.

Jessica fought the urge to reach out and touch the angry-looking welts. 'Aren't they sore?' she asked, wondering how Honey had managed to lie on her back with any degree of comfort.

'Of course. What would be the point of them if they weren't? No, I think I've got just as lucky as you in my own way, Jessica. I've found a master who's determined to keep me in line, which means I'm going to have so much fun proving to him that he can't.' She raked an appraising gaze along the length of Jessica's body. 'That's a great swimsuit, by the way.'

'Thank you,' Jessica said, 'though when I packed it, I was kind of hoping Max would be the one who'd get the benefit of seeing me in it.'

'Well, he should be here very soon. Rafael went to fetch him for a game of beach tennis.'

'Tennis?' Jessica couldn't keep the surprise from her voice. She'd never known Max do anything more energetic on a beach than turn the pages of the latest John Grisham thriller.

'Oh sweetie, you've really never seen your husband flex his muscles among the other alpha males, have you? Any excuse for a contest and they all pile in. It's partly why Damon likes to auction us girls off – the men get so competitive fighting to own us, it raises more money for that charity of his. But you should know all about that, seeing just how much the lovely Jason paid to get his hands on your virgin charms ...'

Jessica glanced over at Jason, wondering whether he'd realised he was being talked about, but he was lying on his back, his hands linked behind his head, oblivious to their conversation. His eyes were hidden behind his dark glasses, and for all she knew he had fallen asleep. Her gaze lit on the bottle of sun lotion, and she realised she hadn't applied any before leaving Jason's suite. If she didn't want to burn under the strong Caribbean sun, she needed to rectify that.

When she picked up the bottle, Honey said, 'Let me do that. Lie down, and I'll make sure I get lotion on that bit in the middle of your back you just can't reach yourself, no matter how flexible you are.'

The woman had a knack of making every sentence, no matter how innocent, sound as though it contained some blatant innuendo, but Jessica obediently lay face down on the towel so Honey could cream her skin. She heard the sound of the bottle being squeezed, then dollops of lotion landed on her back and Honey began to rub them in. Her hands were soft, moving in slow, swirling motions that were deliciously soothing, and for the first time since she'd arrived on the island, Jessica felt herself truly relax. Her eyes closed, and she rested her head on her folded arms, sure that much more of this treatment would lull her to sleep. Only when her friend's hands moved onto the swell of her buttock did she find herself tensing; the touch seemed so intimate in comparison to what had gone before. Yet what could she expect, when the material of her swimsuit was little more than a thin strip bisecting her bum cheeks? She needed the protection of the lotion, after all.

Letting her defences down, she didn't protest at first when Honey worked her fingers ever lower, skimming over the crotch of her swimsuit. The first touch she brushed off as an accident, Honey just growing a little too enthusiastic in her attempts to make sure Jessica's skin was effectively coated with the lotion. When she felt that touch a second time, lingering a little longer, she knew it had been deliberate.

'Honey, I don't think you should be –'

'Shush, Jessie, you know you need this,' Honey replied, easing her finger beneath the edge of the swimsuit so it rested on her wet pussy. And she was wet; whether it was still the residue of her excitement at having Jason come in her mouth, or whether her body was just reacting instinctively to Honey's calculated caresses, she didn't know. Neither, she was shocked to realise, did she particularly care.

Another finger joined the first, and the pads of both digits described lazy circles on Jessica's clit. She bit back a whimper of need, afraid that any noise might wake Jason – if indeed he really was asleep – and get them both into trouble. Whatever he'd brought her down to the beach for, she was damn sure it wasn't to let her mischievous roommate finger-fuck her.

'Look who's arrived, Jessie,' Honey murmured, never pausing in her relentless digital exploration of Jessica's sex.

Glancing up, Jessica saw Max ambling across the sand towards the spot where they lay, in the company of Rafael Dos Santos. He clutched a black plastic tennis racket in his hand, and he looked fresh and relaxed in a short-sleeved shirt and knee-length khaki shorts.

'Stop it, Honey,' she hissed. 'I can't let Max see me like this.' Doing her best to wriggle away from Honey's probing fingers, she hauled herself upright, trying to make it seem as though the two of them were simply chatting and enjoying the sunshine. As she moved, she was horrified to realise that while she'd been half-dozing, Honey must have undone the halter fastening of her swimsuit. The result was that the fabric fell away when she sat up, faster than her clutching hands could stop it, exposing her breasts to the approaching men. Even though one of them was her husband, who'd seen her naked so many times, she still felt embarrassed about having so much of herself on display, especially as her nipples were poking forward jauntily. Why did everyone on this wretched island seem so determined to wrong-foot her at every turn?

'Jessica, what exactly are you doing?' Jason's voice was sharp behind her. She turned in his direction, knowing she was now treating him to the sight of her bare tits.

'I'm sorry, master, I –' Again she found herself apologising for something that couldn't really be her fault, but it was hard to concentrate when Honey was still surreptitiously playing with her pussy.

The sly movements of Honey's fingers hadn't gone totally unnoticed, it seemed. 'Hey, slut, cut that out!' Dos Santos ordered in his rich, Spanish-accented tone.

'I don't know what you're talking about, sir,' Honey said artlessly. Jessica couldn't understand her behaviour. Orders were to be obeyed – her own master had made that very clear to her – yet her friend seemed to revel in doing the exact opposite of what she'd been told.

In a couple of furious strides, Dos Santos covered the stretch of beach between himself and the two women. Reaching down, he grasped hold of Honey's fingers, which seemed to ease out of Jessica's pussy with an audible squelch.

'Look at this!' He held the offending hand up in the air, so everyone could see how its fingers glistened with Jessica's juices. Dos Santos sniffed them, then licked them clean, visibly savouring the taste. Jessica wanted the sand to swallow her up, so mortified was she at realising everyone now knew just how turned on she'd been by Honey's touch.

'If I hadn't stopped you, you'd have made this little trollop come, wouldn't you? How dare you, when you know the only one you're supposed to give pleasure to is your lord and master?' Dos Santos rumbled on. 'It seems the caning I gave you last night hasn't had the desired effect of beating some sense into you, and further punishment is required.' He turned to Max. '*Señor*, I'm afraid we must postpone our game of tennis until later. I need to discipline this wayward brat.'

With that, he hauled Honey up by one arm and began to lead her indoors. The almost bare cheeks of her bottom and her big breasts, so inadequately confined in the skimpy bikini, jiggled with every step she took. Jessica couldn't help but notice that Max's gaze seemed almost magnetised to the sway of Honey's arse, with the marks of her recent punishment so prominent across it.

'So, what shall we do about you?' Jason asked, fixing Jessica with a stern glare and pulling the focus of her attention to him. 'After all, I didn't notice you telling Honey to stop.'

'Master, it wasn't my fault, really it wasn't,' Jessica blustered. 'I only expected her to rub sun lotion on my skin. That's all she said she was going to do. I didn't think she'd start touching my –' She stopped, hoping he'd get the point.

'Touching your what, girl?'

'My – you know, my pussy,' she said at length.

Jason laughed. 'How coy. But that's not the word I expect my girl to use. So why don't you call it what it really is?'

Jessica felt her cheeks burn with shame, but she managed to force out her reply. 'She was touching my cunt, master. And what's more, I was enjoying it.'

'I thought so. And what happens to naughty girls who let themselves be played with in public?'

'They get punished.'

'Indeed they do. And what's more, they get punished in front of their husband, so he can see just how much work he's going to have to put in if he wants to keep them in line.'

She supposed it was inevitable, given that the whole purpose of this week was to turn her into a well-behaved submissive who would do exactly as Max told her. But it would still be so embarrassing to have him witness Jason dealing with her as if she was a misbehaving child. 'I'm sorry, master. I'll do whatever you say. Please don't punish me.'

'It's too late for apologies, girl. You're going over my knee.'

'What, here?' The words slipped out before she could

stop them. It was a reasonable comment, given that there appeared to be nowhere on this long, flat stretch of beach apart from the none-too-solid sun loungers where he could sit and make a lap on which to balance her, but she knew it could only sound as though she was questioning his authority.

'No, you'll be punished in my room. And just for your cheek, I'll use something more severe than the flat of my hand. Max, if you'd like to come with us …'

With that, Jason dragged her to her feet. Holding tight to one of her wrists, he started to march purposefully into the resort building, making her hurry to keep up with him. Max followed a pace behind, and Jessica wondered whether he was watching the movements of her arse, as he'd done with Honey. Jason hadn't given her time to readjust her swimsuit, and the loose material flapped around her waist, making her look and feel more ridiculous than she already did. They passed one of the maids responsible for housekeeping in the corridor close to Jason's room, and though the girl said nothing, other than bobbing her head and offering a respectful, 'Sir,' to Jason and Max, the smile on her face as she regarded Jessica made it clear she had a very good idea of what might be about to happen to her.

Once in the room, Jason took charge. 'Max, if you'd be so kind, there should be a rubber paddle in that selection box of toys Damon leaves in the nightstand. If you could dig that out for me while I sort this bad girl out, I'd appreciate it.'

Again, she was being discussed as though she wasn't important enough to be directly involved in the conversation. Did her master know how demeaning she found that – and how shamefully thrilling?

While Max rootled around in the nightstand, Jason sat down on the low sofa, and ordered Jessica to get over his knee. Much as she wanted to string out the moment before she would have to present herself for punishment, she simply couldn't do it – not when her master seemed determined to raise the stakes every time she did something to displease him. And a rubber paddle didn't sound so bad, not compared to the cane Dos Santos had used on Honey's backside. How much could something like that actually hurt?

'Here we go,' Max said. Jessica heard the sound of a drawer shutting. From her upside-down position on Jason's lap, she watched her husband approach, carrying something which he slapped against his left palm in experimental fashion. 'I have to say that Damon really does think of everything, doesn't he?'

'He certainly does,' Jason replied, taking the paddle from Max. 'You can pull up a chair if you like, but you'll probably get the best view if you sit to my side on the sofa. That way you'll really be able to appreciate how her arse colours.'

Jessica didn't see Max sit down, but she heard the springs of the sofa creak slightly as he took a seat to Jason's right. That meant he was sitting by her feet, rather than her head, with a perfect view of her bottom.

'Right, let's get this out of the way ...' As Jason spoke, he was reaching underneath her body, to catch hold of her swimsuit and edge it down. It seemed a superfluous gesture, given that her bum was already fully on display thanks to the thong design of the suit, but it seemed he wanted the garment pulled down around her knees, the elasticated fabric acting as a kind of impromptu restraint.

'Very nice,' she heard Max murmur, and realised he must be looking at her wet pussy lips where they peeped out from between her thighs. She remembered how he'd suggested spanking her with Mickey, his chauffeur, in attendance, and how her show of contrition had caused him to send the man away. Could he have known that, before too long, he'd find himself in the position of the excited voyeur, waiting for her punishment to be dished out by a man who wouldn't let her apologies change his course of action?

'Now, I don't suppose you're familiar with the paddle –' For the first time since they'd entered the room, Jason was addressing her directly, though she knew he could just as well be talking to Max. 'So take a good look at it before we begin.'

He held the implement under her nose. It was roughly the same size and shape as a table tennis bat, but made of black rubber about an inch thick. More solid than she'd expected, but still she didn't view it as anything to be afraid of.

'And one last thing. I don't intend to give you more swats with this paddle than I think you can take, but if it does become too much for you, just say "violets". That will be our safeword. Use it, and I stop at once. Is that understood?'

'Perfectly, master.' She had no idea why he'd chosen such a random word, but she supposed it wasn't the kind of thing she would otherwise blurt out in the heat of a punishment.

'So, are you ready for this, Jessica?' he asked.

How could she ever be ready to beaten? She wasn't Simone, who welcomed the lash of a whip with almost religious fervour, or Honey, who could find endless ways of manipulating a situation in order to earn a dose of chastisement. She was just an ordinary woman – if ordinary meant stretching her husband's patience to the point where he believed handing her over to another man to be disciplined was the only answer. 'Yes, master,' she replied meekly.

Her master tapped the paddle against each of her cheeks in turn. Gentle taps, they barely registered on her consciousness. It didn't occur to her that he was merely measuring his aim until it was too late, and when the thick rubber bat slapped against her with the full force of his arm behind it, she was completely unprepared.

'Ow, that really hurt!' she yelped, trying to rise up from his lap. Jason's firm hand in the small of her back kept her in position.

'It was supposed to,' came the matter-of-fact reply. 'If it doesn't hurt, you don't learn. And that's what this is all about, right?'

'Yes, master.'

'Now be a good girl, and this will all be over soon.'

There was no way she could endure more than a handful of strokes from that thing. How had she ever thought it was some innocent alternative to a spanking? As the paddle fell again and again, she seemed to feel a dull ache spreading all the way through her bottom. Its broad, round surface slammed into both of her cheeks with every swat, piling pain upon pain. She writhed on Jason's lap, feeling the solid length of his cock beneath her, separated from her bare flesh by only the thickness of his shorts. When Max had spanked her, she'd wanted him to fuck her afterwards, but he'd refused her the pleasure. What would happen this time? Would Jason take her, or Max – or both of them? Each of those scenarios was appealing in its own way, and she tried to think about them to take her mind off the agony of being paddled.

'Are – you – sorry – girl?' Jason asked, the words punctuated by hard slaps of the paddle against her tormented flesh. Her bottom felt as though it was scorching hot, and the blows must surely be turning her skin black and blue. She wanted to kick her legs, to try to disperse the painful sensations, but the swimsuit had effectively hobbled them, restricting her movements. It meant she could only wriggle, rubbing herself against Jason's erection as she did. And God only knew what kind of display she was giving Max.

When she didn't immediately answer, he repeated the four words, and the four slaps, even harder than before, if that was possible.

Tears sprang to her eyes. 'Yes, master,' she sobbed. 'I was wrong to let Honey lead me astray. I'll be good from now on, honestly I will.'

'That's all I needed to hear.' He brought the paddle round to her face. 'Now, I want you to kiss this and thank me for chastising you.'

She pressed her lips to the rubber, finding it hot to the touch. 'Thank you, master, for punishing me, and for letting my husband watch you at work,' she said.

'Good girl,' he murmured, close to her ear, the words a soothing balm to her soul. She was his good girl; she'd taken everything he'd given her and hadn't even thought of using her safeword. And now, surely, she would be receive the reward that came from obeying him.

He helped her to stand, and she glanced from him to Max. Both men had prominent bulges in their shorts, and she couldn't wait to give them the relief they must need.

Immediately, Jason dashed her hopes. 'Max and I are going down to the bar,' he said. 'We have things to discuss. Until we return, I want you to stand in the corner over there, with your face to the wall and your hands on your head. You can think on what you've done, and consider how to rectify your behaviour in future. And if I find out you've moved in my absence, I'll repeat the punishment you've just received.'

She wanted to ask how long he might be away, but decided against voicing the question, reckoning that if she did, his response would be more swats of that infernal paddle. He hadn't given her permission to pull up her swimsuit, or remove it entirely, so she was forced to waddle over to the corner.

Max muttered something to Jason which she didn't quite hear. The response was a short burst of laughter. Then the door clicked shut, and Jessica was left alone to wait for her master's return.

Chapter Eleven

Max followed Jason out of the room. This wasn't how he'd envisaged Jessica's punishment ending, with her being left to reflect on her misbehaviour. She'd looked so gorgeous, so vulnerable with her bare bottom stained a fiery red, and he'd longed to pull her to him and kiss the marks of her tears from her cheeks. That, he now understood, was the real power the dominant held in this situation; the power to break someone down to their basic essence, then put them back together again. The power to hurt, and to heal. Wielded in the correct manner, it could only strengthen the bond he shared with his wife.

Maybe that was what Jason wanted to talk to him about, to see what he'd learned from watching Jessica having her arse paddled. And though he hadn't wanted a drink when the punishment had begun, he was certainly in need of one now. His cock had risen to full attention as he'd witnessed Jessica's humiliation, and it hadn't yet begun to subside. When he'd encouraged the other man to bid for her services, he hadn't realised it would mean he wouldn't get to fuck her until the week was over and she was returned to him, a suitably contrite submissive. Sure, there was any number of house girls on hand, all of them willing to pleasure any of the male guests with whichever orifice was required, but it wasn't the same as sinking your cock into your own wife and hearing her scream out her love and gratitude as she came.

The bar area was surprisingly busy. Glancing at his watch, Max saw it was half-past 12; perhaps a few pre-lunch aperitifs were being taken.

Jason had caught the barman's attention. 'I'll have a beer, please. And Max ...?'

'Gin and tonic, thanks.' He couldn't remember the last time he'd had a G and T, and he reckoned the barman, trained, like all Barada's staff, to the highest standards of service and hospitality, would be capable of producing a pretty good one.

'So,' Jason asked, while they waited for their drinks, 'how was it for you?'

Max considered his reply. At length, he said, 'I think I'm beginning to understand it, the contract between dominant and submissive. What each expects from the other, and what the rules are. And I'm starting to discover things about myself I didn't know, desires I've somehow kept repressed for a long time. But what about you, Jason? I mean, you're what? Thirty?'

'Twenty-nine.'

'See, you're more than 20 years younger than me, but you're so confident in this world, so sure of what you want, and what you want your women to be. But when did you first realise you were a dominant?'

The barman interrupted before Jason could answer, setting a white paper coaster down in front of Max and placing his gin and tonic in front of them. A wedge of lime floated in the glass, and Max used a swizzle stick to agitate the drink, watching bubbles rise to the surface. He took a sip, enjoying the sharp, quinine bite of the tonic. Until that moment, he hadn't realised quite how dry his mouth had grown, watching Jason paddle Jessica's bottom.

Jason took a swig of his beer, and wiped foam from his lips with the back of his hand. 'I think, ever since I first started taking a serious interest in women, I've always been excited by the thought of them being tied up and made to do things. When I surfed for porn online, those were always the images I lingered over longest, and I bought a couple of books of spanking stories that I read and re-read so many times the pages eventually fell out. But the first woman I ever punished, well …'

He took another drink, his eyes taking on a faraway quality, as though he was recalling events that Max suspected were never too far from the front of his mind.

'Tell me about her,' he prompted.

'When I was 19, I used to train in a gym that was owned by an old boxing promoter. You wouldn't know his name, but you'd recognise a couple of the lads he coached. Anyway, his wife, Christine, used to help out in the place, doing his paperwork, and she was a real stunner. Blonde, legs all the way up to her arse, and she always dressed in really short, tight skirts that showed her figure off to best advantage. All the lads used to fantasise about bending her over the ropes and giving her a good seeing-to, but for some reason she took a real shine to me.'

Max knew Jason wouldn't need too much in the way of encouragement to spill all the details, but the feel of his reviving hard-on prompted him to mutter, 'Go on.'

'She cornered me one night, when I was the last one in the gym. Her old man had gone home, and she told me she needed help with some heavy equipment that he'd neglected to put away. Well, of course I was happy to oblige, but while I'd got my hands full shifting a set of dumbbells, she put her hands down my shorts and told me she needed to be fucked.'

'And you obliged her there, as well?'

'Are you kidding? She was putting it all on a plate and I didn't know how to resist. And even if I had, I wouldn't have wanted to. It's your classic Mrs Robinson story – experienced older woman seduces naïve but very willing young man.'

Max found himself wondering how this had caused Jason to realise he was dominant, given this particular Mrs Robinson sounded like she'd been thoroughly in control of the situation. The younger man's next words answered that question.

'The next time Christine made a move, she took a completely different tack. She told me she'd been such a naughty girl, sleeping with me behind her husband's back. I thought this meant he'd found out, and I was in for a real pasting, but instead she said the only way she could atone for it was if I was to punish her. And by punish, she meant spank.

'Well, just like the previous occasion, she made sure the two of us were the only ones left in the gym. I think the fact we were doing it there added to the thrill for her, almost like she was hoping someone might come back for some reason and catch us in the act. Anyway, she persuaded me that she needed to have her bare bottom spanked. And the moment she got over my knee and I started edging her little pink panties down, it was like all the stories I'd ever read had come to life. Having her there, waiting for me to bring my hand down on her arse, it just felt *right*, you know? Like this was what I'd been born to do.

'I spanked her hard and I spanked her fast, not knowing anything about varying the pace or building up the intensity. And she was wriggling and gasping and telling me what a bad, naughty, dirty girl she'd been, and how she'd never do it again ... God, Max, I was as hard as a rock.'

That pretty much described his own condition right at this moment, Max thought, gulping at his G and T. Hard and in need of someone – anyone – to ease the ache in his groin. But there was still a little more of Jason's story to come before he could make any attempt to seek relief.

'By the time I'd finished, her arse was glowing beetroot, and when I rubbed it, it was so hot to the touch. My palm was red and stinging, but I felt such a sense of satisfaction. Christine was sobbing and panting and begging me to fuck her, so I did. To be honest, I only lasted a few strokes, I was so worked up, and when I came, I shot my come all over her bum cheeks, long, creamy strings all over that bright red flesh.'

'And did you keep on seeing her after that?'

Jason shook his head. 'Turns out her old man really had got wind she was screwing around behind his back, but he thought it was one of the other lads down the gym. I thought getting involved with her any further would be way too dangerous, even though I'd have loved to spank that gorgeous bare arse of hers again. I suppose it's because she was the first that I've always had a thing about dominating older women. But after that, I started getting into the fetish club scene, and meeting women there. That's pretty much it, until I got the chance to come here, and things moved on to a whole new level.'

'So tell me,' Max said. 'What's it like fucking Jessica when you've got her arse all red and sore?'

Jason shrugged. 'You know what? I haven't actually fucked her yet. I suppose I'm working my way up to that pleasure. But she does give a beautiful blowjob. Though I reckon I must be bigger than she's used to, because she really has to stretch her lips round my –'

He broke off, no doubt realising what he'd just implied. At least he had the grace to look a little embarrassed, though Max's reaction on learning that his wife was in the hands of someone who was considerably better endowed than himself was one of envy mixed with a strong desire to see Jessica writhing on the end of Jason's dick.

He was distracted by some kind of commotion on the other side of the room. Three or four men appeared to be standing round in a half-circle, their backs obstructing his view of whatever had so obviously captured their attention.

He gestured to the barman, who ambled over, prepared to receive an order for a fresh round of drinks. 'The same again, please,' Max said, surprised to discover he'd finished his G and T while listening to Jason's story. 'And you don't know what's happening over there, do you?'

The barman craned his neck to see. 'Looks like Mr Radford's about to make some girl ride the Beast.'

'The Beast?' Max enquired. 'And what the hell's that when it's at home?'

'Let me make your drink, sir, then I suggest you wander over and take a look. It'll be worth it, I assure you.'

When Max had a fresh gin and tonic to hand, and Jason another beer, they did as the barman suggested. They found themselves standing at the side of Sebastian Voller, whose blond hair already seemed to have lightened and his tan deepened under the influence of the Caribbean sun. Max once more offered silent thanks to Jason for helping keep Jessica out of the man's clutches.

'Come to join in the fun, eh?' Voller asked, his tone surprisingly civil to Max's ears.

'The barman said something about the Beast. Do you know what that is, exactly?' Max said.

'One of Barada's favourite toys, and mine,' Voller replied, waving a hand towards what stood in front of the expectant group of men. 'Take a good look. I'm sure you'll work out how it gets its name.'

What Max saw reminded him of nothing so much as a bucking bronco machine, with its sturdy body designed for one person to comfortably straddle. However, where the bronco was designed to swivel and rock and unseat its rider, this appeared to be anchored more securely in place. And instead of a saddle, something far more erotic protruded from its back – a dildo of almost freakish proportions that he estimated to be a good nine inches long, and as thick as his wrist. Sinuous veins adorned its length, and it already glistened with a thick coating of lubricant.

To the side of the Beast stood Joe Radford, the oil baron who'd been one of Max's dinner companions the previous night. The garrulous Texan had spoken at length about his desire to buy one of the other men's wives in the auction and treat her to his own brand of Southern hospitality, and he'd succeeded in acquiring the pneumatic Adele Quinn. She stood next to Joe now, looking down at the floor, naked but for a striking clear plastic collar around her neck, and matching cuffs on her wrists and ankles.

'All right, gentlemen, who would like to see this wayward little slut ride the Beast?' Joe asked. His question was greeted by a chorus of raucous cheers. 'Very well then, darlin', I want y'all to get up on that thing and show these nice gentlemen how much of that big, thick dick you can fit in your snatch.'

Beside Max, Voller sighed. 'Americans, always such buffoons.'

Max said nothing, though he suspected that if Voller was charge of this scene, he would have cut out all the preamble and placed the girl on the contraption forcibly. Just looking at the size of the dildo told him this was something to be approached with care, and mounted at the submissive's own pace.

Adele climbed up onto the Beast, bracing her feet on the thin platforms on either side of the solid bulk of the machine. She poised herself over the dildo, appearing to take a deep breath as she mentally considered the prospect of sinking down on the mighty rod. She'll never be able to take it, Max thought, looking at the girl's petite body. There's no way such an immense thing can fit inside her.

An expectant hush gripped the watching men as Adele held her pussy lips apart and began to sink down. Her eyes were closed and her face bore an expression of Zen-like calm as the dildo slowly disappeared inside her. Max yearned to step right up to the Beast, so he could have the best possible view of the fake cock cleaving its way into Adele's soft depths. It must be really stretching her wide, and he wondered how she bore the sensation in almost total silence. Only the occasional gasp gave an indication that she was feeling any kind of strain. His skin flushed hot, and his cock, which had finally begun to subside after the excitement created by watching Jason punishing Jessica, reared up as hard as before. Discreetly, he adjusted himself in his shorts, though when he looked around he couldn't help but notice that already one or two of the other men were making no effort to hide their arousal, stroking themselves openly over their clothing.

When as much of the plastic rod as she could possibly take had lodged itself in Adele's channel – and Max was stunned to notice that less than a couple of inches of the rude, flesh-coloured thing were still visible from between the girl's splayed thighs – a smattering of applause broke out.

'Wow!' Jason muttered beside him, his voice strained and husky. 'I really didn't think that was possible.'

'Don't let the little slut's appearance fool you,' Voller retorted. 'I've seen her take an entire fist up her pussy, and another up her arse, before now. Nothing is too much for her. Mind you, who can be surprised she'll offer herself to anyone when her husband can only get it up if he takes one of those little blue pills beforehand, hey?'

'Thank you all, gentlemen,' Joe Radford was saying, 'thank you kindly. But that's only part one of the performance. You can see how snugly this wicked little darlin' fits on the Beast, but what's going to happen when she starts to ride it?'

For the first time, Max realised that the Texan held in his hand a remote control, not dissimilar to the one he used at home to change the channels on the TV. He pressed one of the buttons, and the dildo juddered into life, beginning to move in a slow, smooth up and down rhythm. Max couldn't help wondering who might have constructed this fucking machine, and whether it had been to Barada's specifications, or whether there was a wider market for these extreme mechanical toys. Jason had mentioned something about visiting fetish clubs, but the expression on his face suggested he'd never seen anything like this there, for he seemed to be equally as enthralled as Max by the sight of the huge artificial dick powering into Adele's cunt. The steady pace of the Beast was clearly causing her no problems, for she moved in time with the thing, caressing her big, firm tits and wiggling her arse, behaving almost as if she was astride a human lover. Max couldn't be entirely sure, but as she hitched herself up slightly, he could swear there was more in the way of lubrication on the mammoth shaft then there had been before, and that Adele's own juices were mingling with the sticky covering that had been applied to help ease her passage onto the thing.

'And now this is where it starts to get interesting,' Voller murmured somewhere beside him. Max was tempted to ask him what he meant, but a moan from Adele captured his attention. Radford had increased the pace of the thrusts, and what had been a gentle ride had become more of a gallop. With every stroke, more of the dildo slithered from her hole, before slamming back in again hard, and he could only imagine how that was stimulating the network of nerves in her vulva. She held on tight to the body of the Beast, squealing and bucking as it fucked her.

Radford stabbed at another button on his remote, and now the dildo gyrated in tight circles, while still hammering in and out of the girl. Years ago, when they'd first become fashionable, Jessica had bought one of those Rabbit vibrators, Max recalled. Its unique selling point had been that it moved in a circular motion no mere man could achieve – or so the girl in the shop had claimed – and now Max saw how that technique might be used to reduce a woman to a state of helpless, sweating, screaming bliss.

For Adele was in bliss, there was no doubt about it. She might be plugged by the biggest dildo he'd ever seen, and that dildo might be reaming her body almost brutally, but he could tell she was loving every moment of this weird, depraved treatment. As if to confirm his thoughts, she threw her head back and yelled out her orgasm, the muscles in her thighs visibly trembling as she did her best to cling to the Beast.

'You see those eyebolts along the side of the machine?' Voller asked, and Max followed his gaze. 'That is so shackles can be attached, so a slave can be tethered to the Beast for as long as her master wishes. You wouldn't believe how many times these little sluts can be made to come – however much they beg to be released.'

Max noticed Jason shoot Voller a look he couldn't quite decipher, but it was enough to convince him his friend had as unfavourable an opinion of the German as he did. If Jessica had fallen into Voller's clutches, would she have been forced to ride the Beast into a state of exhaustion? He was glad he wasn't likely to find out, even though the image of her gripping the thing with her thighs while the dildo jackhammered into her caused his cock to lurch with lust. He needed to attend to himself, and soon. Glancing round the room, it seemed a couple of the others had felt the need even more strongly, for they had their cocks in their hands and were stealthily wanking.

Adele cried out as her pleasure peaked again, before slumping forward on the machine. That seemed to signal the end of the performance, for Radford fiddled with the remote and the dildo first stopped rotating, then slowed in pace before coming to a gradual halt. Extending a hand, showing her some real tenderness for the first time since he'd ordered her to mount the Beast, Radford helped her to climb off it.

Conscious the show was over, the audience began to drift away in the direction of the dining area. Max noticed Malcolm Quinn, Adele's husband, sitting in a low-backed leather and chrome chair, his expression one of pride and satisfaction. He must have been there the whole time, concealed by the other members of the audience, watching on as his young wife was put through her paces.

'Sir.' The voice was gentle in Max's ear, and he turned to see one of the house girls smiling at him. He couldn't remember her name, but she was a pretty enough thing, with brown hair piled in messy curls on top of her head, and breasts that strained at the fastening of her uniform dress. 'You look as though you're in need of some relief.'

As she spoke, she popped open a couple of the fasteners that ran the length of her dress, revealing a mouth-watering glimpse of creamy cleavage. Another couple, and her bare breasts were fully on display to him, their fat red nipples hard and enticing. How sweet it would be, Max thought, to slide his cock into the channel between those gorgeous tits, and let her wrap the soft flesh around his straining shaft. Just what he needed after everything he'd witnessed so far today.

'You have some fun with her,' Jason said, as if reading his mind. 'I'll go and deal with Jessica. She'll have had more than enough time to reflect on what a naughty girl she's been.'

Max had no idea what dealing with Jessica might involve, but as the house girl unfastened the rest of her dress to show him she was completely naked beneath it, he found he didn't really care. All that mattered was letting this girl give him the tit-fuck he craved. Not caring who might be watching, he let her take him by the hand and lead him over to a low couch, so she could get down on her knees before him and attend to him in all the ways he enjoyed most.

Chapter Twelve

Jessica didn't look round when she heard the door click open, knowing that doing so would probably earn her another couple of swats on an arse that still ached from her earlier paddling. She waited for the sound of her master's voice, but instead it was a woman who spoke, her tone melodious, her accent unmistakably French. '*Bonjour*, housekeeping!' The cheerful words were accompanied by the rattling and clanking of a metal trolley being pushed into the room.

Wasn't the standard etiquette for chambermaids to knock first, then withdraw if it became clear the guest didn't wish to be disturbed at that particular moment? Perhaps, Jessica reflected, but nothing followed the usual standards in Damon Barada's establishment; everything was skewed to increase the possibility that some poor unfortunate like herself might be caught in a compromising act. She had no idea what the staff here earned; indeed, she could very well imagine there might be submissive women who would pay for the thrill of being dominated and fucked by Barada and his wealthy colleagues. What she had no doubt of was that coming upon a scene such as the maid had discovered here – Jessica standing obediently in the corner with her hands on her head and her swimsuit bunched around her ankles, her bum cheeks bearing the vivid marks of a recent punishment – would be classed as one of the perks of the job.

'Oh my goodness, what do we have here?' the maid asked. 'It looks like someone's been a very naughty girl, hasn't she?'

Jessica only knew the girl had come to her when she felt soft breath against her ear, and smelled lily-of-the-valley perfume; her shoes had made no sound on the polished wooden floorboards.

'Your poor bottom must be very sore, *madame*,' the maid continued. 'Oh *ma pauvre petite*, you must have done something very bad to earn such a beating.'

But I didn't, Jessica wanted to point out. All I did was let Honey rub lotion into my skin so I didn't burn in the sun. I know that when she started touching me where she shouldn't have, I should have stopped her, but I didn't because it felt so good. However, she knew better than to explain anything to this girl, to try to turn and make the case for her defence. For all she knew, the maid would immediately go scurrying off to find her master, and tell him she'd spoken out of turn. She could only imagine how painful the consequences of that might be.

'Let me attend to you, *madame*. It will only take a moment, and I can help ease the ache in that oh so red bottom of yours.'

The maid stepped away. Jessica kept her eyes fixed to the wall, trying to gauge what the girl might be doing from the noises she made. She appeared to be opening and closing drawers, presumably rifling through Jason's nightstand in search of something. Jessica's stomach lurched. Please God, she thought, don't let her be looking for something in that toy box Damon provides.

When the maid returned to her side, Jessica heard a sound she hadn't been expecting – the lid of a jar being unscrewed – and felt a cool substance being applied to the surface of her arse. She hissed out a grateful breath as the maid smoothed the balm, or whatever it was, over her inflamed flesh. For someone whose job involved cleaning the resort bedrooms, the girl's hands were deliciously soft. Maybe she wore rubber gloves when she worked, Jessica considered, her mind racing as she wondered what it might feel like to be caressed by fingers sheathed in thick latex, to have them pushing up into both her holes, exploring her front and back. What's wrong with me? she wondered. Why does everything that happens to me these days make me think of the kinkiest possibilities, the most outrageous behaviour?

It wasn't all that surprising, she supposed, not when the maid's fingers were moving over the crown of her buttock, closer and closer to the cleft dividing her cheeks. If they travelled any lower, they would brush dangerously close to her sex lips, just as Honey's had done. And if that happened, she knew, just knew, that she would make no effort to stop this girl in her explorations. Until she'd set foot on Isla Barada, she'd barely even contemplated the prospect of letting another woman finger her pussy, and bring her to the brink of climax with skilful touches to her clit – now, twice in less than the space of a day, she had given herself over without a murmur to these insistent Sapphic caresses.

The soft pad of a finger was trailed over the seam of Jessica's nether lips. She shivered, wanting more but not daring to speak and break her master's rule. Surely her reaction must be letting the maid know just where she needed to be touched, and how little of that treatment it would take to tip her over into orgasm.

'Maybe *madame* might care to spread her stance a little further,' the maid suggested. 'That way I can make sure I have creamed all your flesh.'

Without hesitation, Jessica shuffled her legs as wide as the restrictive grip of the swimsuit would allow. It only widened the gap between them by a matter of inches, but it was an unspoken invitation to the maid to slip her hand into that humid space at the apex of her thighs.

Again, those wicked fingers brushed over her pouting pussy, but now they lingered, caressing the smoothly shaven flesh and applying the most delicate of touches to her clit. Long-delayed pleasure after the pain her master had inflicted, and all the sweeter for being provoked in her by a woman who, she was certain, must know exactly how it felt to be on the receiving end of a sustained paddling. Her sigh was deep, heartfelt, and she would have broken her express instruction not to turn her head to look directly at the girl who was stimulating her so beautifully if the door hadn't swung open at that moment.

'What on earth is going on here?' Jason bellowed.

Caught with her fingers in the cookie jar, the maid withdrew her hand from between Jessica's legs and began to explain her actions. '*Pardon, monsieur*, I was only trying to soothe the beautiful bottom of your slave. I did not mean to –'

Jason cut her apology short. 'That's as may be, but I

decide what attention Jessica receives, and when. And if I were going to apply something to her arse, I certainly wouldn't be using this.'

With her face to the wall, Jessica couldn't see what was happening, but the maid's anguished little cry suggested to her that the jar of balm had been snatched from her fingers. 'Do you know how much this moisturiser costs, girl? You must have used half the pot.'

'Oh *monsieur*, I didn't realise. If I had known, I would have –'

Jessica tuned out the maid's pleading. She would never have imagined that Jason, who looked as though he shaved on those occasions when he remembered, and seemed uncomfortable in anything more formal than a T-shirt, would use facial moisturiser. Maybe she'd got it wrong about his choice of career; she'd originally believed he was one of Barada's employees playing a part, a thought she'd quickly dismissed, but maybe he was a professional actor, and that's why he was vain enough to slather expensive potions on his skin. It would explain why he could slip so easily into the role of the stern dominant who expected nothing other than to be obeyed.

His voice snapped her back to full awareness of the situation.

'Sorry isn't good enough, girl. I should speak to Damon, get the cost of the cream deducted from your wages.' His reaction seemed over the top, but Jessica suspected the threat was designed to get the girl to do whatever it took to resolve the matter here and now. If that was indeed the case, it had worked.

'No, please, *monsieur*,' the maid whimpered. 'Please

don't speak to Monsieur Barada. He will dismiss me on the spot, and then I will have to go back home to Lille. It is so grey there, so dull, and I love working here so much.'

'You should have thought of that before you started taking liberties with my property.'

Jessica couldn't decide whether Jason was referring to the moisturiser, or herself.

'I know, *monsieur*, but I could not help myself. I saw such a delicious bottom, in need of attention ... It was too much to resist. And I will take whatever punishment you see fit, just as long as you don't tell Monsieur Barada what I have done.'

'Very well – what's your name?' Jason asked.

'Nathalie, monsieur.'

'Very well, Nathalie, let's have you over my knee. Jessica, you may turn round. I'd like you to witness this.'

Jessica did an obedient pirouette, hands still linked together behind her head, even though she felt a slight burn between her shoulder blades from the strain of keeping her arms in the same position for so long. It didn't surprise her that her master wanted her to watch Nathalie being punished. Humiliating as it was to have your bottom smacked, it was ten times worse when someone else was there to see that bottom turn red beneath a punishing palm, and hear every last sob and plea for mercy.

Jason settled himself on the edge of the bed, patting the top of his leg and encouraging Nathalie to arrange herself on his lap. She did so without a murmur, lying face down, her rump squarely over Jason's thick thighs.

For the first time, Jessica got a good look at the girl. Barely into her 20s, her black hair had been fastened into a high ponytail, and she wore the plain white tunic which was the regulation outfit for the resort's maids. Her long legs were bare, and the flat, raffia soles of her white shoes explained why she'd been able to move so noiselessly across the floor.

'Right, let's get this over with.' With quick, efficient movements, he inched Nathalie's tunic up till it was around her waist, revealing a small, round bottom covered by high-waisted white panties – practical, but not in the least glamorous. The granny panties seemed to offend Jason's aesthetic sensibilities, as he reached to take them off.

'Oh *non, monsieur*,' Nathalie begged. 'Please don't bare my bottom, please. I couldn't bear the shame of it.'

Jason was deaf to her entreaties. Fingers hooked in the waistband, he pulled the knickers down, revealing the olive-toned contours of Nathalie's arse. As Nathalie spread her legs, helping him in the ease of their removal even as she whined and pleaded for him not to take her underwear off, Jessica couldn't help noticing that the girl's lower lips were thickly covered with bushy hair. It even seemed to extend up into the crack of her arse. Not that she was an expert in such matters, but she didn't believe she'd ever seen such a hairy pussy, and for some reason the sight intrigued her. She wanted to step closer and take a better look, but Jason hadn't given her permission to approach, so she stayed where she was.

'I'll make this quick and sharp, so you don't forget your lesson,' Jason informed Nathalie. With that, he raised his hand and began to spank her. Over and over his palm descended, slapping each of the girl's buttocks in turn. His movements were rapid, never giving her time to recover from one swat before the next was on its punishing way. Every smack seemed loud, even in such a big and airy room, and each one was answered with a little yelp from Nathalie.

For the first time, Jessica was able to see the effect a hard spanking had on an unprotected bottom. Nathalie's skin blushed a deeper crimson with every stroke, mottling and taking on an angry red look. If she were able to reach out and touch it, Jessica swore she would be able to feel the heat suffusing those poor, abused cheeks.

But for all the pain Nathalie must be experiencing, there had to be pleasure building too. Jessica knew all too well how the heat generated by every spank could find its way to a girl's pussy, deep and sweet and bringing with it the promise of an orgasm to come – if she were lucky enough to be allowed such an indulgence by her master. Nathalie's writhings on Jason's lap had taken on a more visibly erotic nature, and Jessica wondered whether the maid was rubbing herself against Jason's big, hard dick. If you were to position yourself just right, she reckoned it would be possible to create enough friction on your clit as you wriggled and squirmed to make yourself come.

Jason seemed to have worked that out too, for abruptly he pushed Nathalie from his lap, sending her sprawling to the floor. 'That's quite enough of that, you little minx.'

The maid raised herself to her knees, making no attempt to adjust her dress. As she moved, Jessica got a good flash of her pussy. It looked swollen and wet; clear evidence that being spanked had turned Nathalie on.

'So, may I go about my duties now, *monsieur*?' Nathalie asked. 'I promise you I will never use anything belonging to any of the guests without asking permission first.'

'No, not yet.' Jason took hold of the maid's hand and guided her to her feet, then arranged her face down over the end of the bed. 'Jessica, come here,' he ordered.

When she did, her progress still hampered by the swimsuit around her ankles, he made her lie down alongside Nathalie. He tugged at the swimsuit, and she kicked her feet out of it on his command, grateful to be free of its constraints at last.

'How very lovely you both look,' he told her. 'Two naughty girls with punished bottoms and wet pussies just aching to be fucked.'

Jessica heard noises that suggested her master was stripping out of his clothes, then the familiar ripping sound as a condom packet was torn open. In moments, he was back beside the two girls, running a hand over each of their bottoms in turn. The little wince Nathalie gave as he caressed her suggested her bottom was considerably tenderer to the touch than Jessica's own.

'Now, the only question is which of you shall I fuck first?'

He seemed to spend for ever considering his options. Jessica fought to retain her self-control, even as she longed to beg him to sink that thick, hard shaft into her depths. She'd lost track of just how much time had passed since Max and Jason had disappeared from the room, but her senses had been on fire for all that time.

Despite the agony she'd endured, the paddling had left her desperate to be fucked, and if her master decided to take Nathalie first, she didn't know if she could stand the frustration.

'Shall it be Jessica, who just can't seem to stop offering herself to any little slut who decides to play with her?' Thrusting a hand between Jessica's legs, he stroked her wet folds, coaxing a whimper of desire from her. 'Or shall it be Nathalie, who doesn't seem to know it's wrong to use someone else's property without their permission?'

Abruptly, he withdrew his probing fingers. Jessica didn't see him bury them in Nathalie's pussy, but the girl's soft cry suggested that was where they'd gone.

'Perhaps I should punish the pair of you again for forcing me to make such an impossible choice?' he mused.

That would be too cruel, and Jessica almost broke down and begged him to penetrate her. She could imagine all too clearly the view he had as he looked down on them: two bare bottoms, one dark, blotchy red, the other fading to a more dusky shade; two pussies, one shaved almost clean, the other a riot of curly hair; two pairs of lusciously dewy lips, designed to be parted by the shaft of a thick, erect penis. It was a sight that would make any man pause, weighing up his options, but the waiting was driving her to distraction.

Jason grasped her firmly by the hip, and she realised he'd made his choice. He guided the head of his cock into place with his other hand, and thrust home. All the while she'd been bent over the bed, her juices had been flowing in anticipation of this moment, and he slid in with ease. If she'd registered a difference in size between him and Max when she'd sucked his cock, that difference became even more pronounced as his thickness pushed the walls of her channel apart. Of all the men she'd been with, maybe one other had been as long, as hefty as this, and she relished the feeling of being taken by something that had the potential to give her the most glorious shafting of her life.

Almost as soon as she'd grown used to the feeling of him there, moving back and forth with slow, shallow strokes, he pulled out, turning his attention to Nathalie. Jessica couldn't resist turning her head to watch the instant of penetration; it might earn her a punishment further down the line, but right now she needed to satisfy her savage curiosity. She'd never seen anyone being fucked mere inches from her face, and for all she knew she would never have the opportunity again.

The French girl groaned as Jason entered her, whimpered as he pushed in further, all the way until his groin seemed to fuse with her punished bum cheeks and she registered the sensation of him pressing against her tenderised flesh. Just as with Jessica, he treated Nathalie to three or four lazy thrusts, then withdrew.

A pattern set, Jason began to alternate from one woman to the other, fucking each of them in turn for a minute or so. Every time, he brought Jessica to a point where she knew a couple more strokes would make her come, from the friction of her pussy rubbing against the bedcover and the sensation of being so widely stretched round his cock, but he seemed to sense the moment at which she was about to cross the threshold, and returned to Nathalie.

Jessica wished she had a mirror to hand, so she could watch the scene, Jason sliding into first one pussy, then the next, over and over. She had to admire his stamina, as he took first one of them, then the other, to the brink of climax time after time, without seemingly coming anywhere near to his own orgasm. Nathalie was clearly suffering more from his teasing treatment than she, for every time he re-entered her, driving in to the hilt, he must have been stoking the fire in her spanked arse. Soon, she was babbling in a mixture of English and French, telling him she would do anything, anything he wanted, if he would only finish the job and make her come.

To the side of her, Nathalie's hand clutched at the bedspread. An unknown impulse compelled Jessica to twine her fingers with the other girl's, giving her some kind of comfort in the throes of her erotic torment. Jason said nothing, but at last he increased his pace, shunting into Nathalie with hard, unrelenting strokes.

'Ah, *mon Dieu*!' Nathalie gasped, as his balls slapped against her bum cheeks. 'It hurts, but it hurts so good.' She gave a tormented little whimper, and grasped Jessica's fingers so hard her knuckles turned white. '*Aiee*!' Her grip relaxed, and Jessica knew she'd come.

Jason, however, had only just started. He took hold of Jessica's hips in both hands this time, pulling her hard onto his groin. Close to his own release now, he fucked her with a power that almost took his breath away. He'd dominated her with his words, and that wicked paddle, and now he was dominating her with his cock, and his desire to possess her, body and soul. All she could do was let him take her where he wanted to go, to some place that seemed outside time, outside all rational thought. The moment he held her tight to him, keeping her still while he pumped his seed into the condom, and ordered her to come for him was the moment her world broke apart and reformed, a little brighter than before. Her orgasm went on until she thought she might pass out from the strength of the waves rolling through her. At last, Jason's cock slipped from her, though her pussy muscles clutched at it as if she couldn't bear to let him leave.

She rolled on to her back, staring up at the ceiling, as Jason ushered Nathalie to the door.

'No, don't put them on,' she heard him say, and in her lust-befuddled state she realised he was talking about the maid's big, unflattering knickers. 'Leave them on the trolley so everyone can see you've been so bad they had to be stripped from you so your wicked little bottom could be spanked. And make sure you go bare under your uniform for the rest of the day. If I bump into you, I'll be sure to put my hand under your skirt to check – and if I touch cotton, rather than soft, wet pussy, you'll be in all kinds of trouble.'

Once Nathalie had wheeled her trolley out of the room, and the door had clicked securely shut behind her, Jason strode back to where Jessica lay on the bed.

'Don't get too comfortable there,' he warned her. 'We have more training to fit in before dinner, you know.'

As Jessica hauled herself into a sitting position, she began to suspect the one thing she would never truly be around her master was comfortable.

Chapter Thirteen

After five days on the island, Jessica felt as though this strange existence, this world where she lived to carry out the orders of a dominant man, compliantly subjugated, was the only one she'd ever known. London, her clubbing adventures, the thrills of hunting young, willing prey; it all seemed like a dream. If it wasn't for the fact she'd spent time with Max since they'd arrived here, she could have believed she'd dreamt him too.

Every night, she slept chained to her master's bed, and every morning she woke to discover what fresh humiliation he had in store for her. He decided what she ate, what she wore, where she went. She could never have imagined that with those choices taken out of her hands she would feel so free.

If he ordered her to drop to the ground and display herself, in the submissive posture he'd taught her on their first night together, she would do so at once, no matter where they were or who else might be in the vicinity. And he trained her in other ways, teaching her to accept the feel of various implements of chastisement, from the soft suede flogger to the vicious, stinging riding crop, the wooden hairbrush to the two-tailed tawse.

Though she couldn't say she enjoyed being spanked,

exactly, she did find she preferred those punishments where she found herself over Jason's lap. There was something so much more intimate about being held in place by one big hand in the small of her back, while the other smacked her bare cheeks. And all the time she was aware of the press of his cock against her belly, haunting her with the promise of what was to come.

At other times, she would be arranged over the whipping stool in Damon's dungeon. She hadn't even known the room existed till Jason signed the key out from reception one afternoon and used it to let the two of them into this very adult playground. When he tired of the stool, he might put her in a faithful reproduction of a mediaeval pillory, her head and hands through the holes and the wooden contraption securely locked so she could not escape while her exposed bottom received a thrashing.

Jason could find an infinite number of reasons to punish her – from spilling food from her breakfast bowl to gossiping with Honey when she happened to run into her friend in the corridor. That chat with Honey, brief as it had been, was an enlightening one. It seemed that only Jessica had the privilege of sleeping at her master's feet; the other slaves were returned to their rooms and shackled by their wrists to the bed, so they weren't able to give in to the temptation to play with themselves. Jessica had made sympathetic noises on hearing this, but was glad she wasn't forced to spend her nights in that narrow bunk in the institution-like room she'd been assigned to share with Honey, restrained and frustrated.

In addition to tutoring her to receive discipline, Jason also introduced Jessica to the art of bondage. The well-stocked toy chest Damon had provided for him contained several lengths of red silken rope, and Jason used them to place her in a hogtie, first binding her wrists and ankles before securing them to each other so she was bent back on herself in a bow. When she was immobilised to his satisfaction, he used his phone to take a couple of photos of her in that position, naked and helpless, and sent them to Max. 'I'm sure he'd love to see how beautiful you look right now,' he commented. Jessica said nothing. Jason had already warned her there was a ball-gag in his box of tricks, and if she spoke out of turn he wouldn't hesitate to use it on her.

When he ordered her to open her mouth, she thought he was indeed about to gag her, although she'd remained silent all through the process of being hogtied, just as he'd demanded. She fought the urge to protest, knowing how unfair it was that she'd obeyed his instructions to the letter and yet he still seemed determined to make her suffer further. To her surprise, the ball-gag stayed in its box. Instead, he dropped his shorts to his ankles, stepped out of them and presented his cock to her lips. She didn't need to be told what to do next. Snaking out her tongue, she swiped it over his helm, licking up the salty drop of precome that beaded at its tip.

Opening wider, she took him inside, relishing the briny taste of him, the uniquely musky scent that rose from the soft mat of hair at his groin. While she sucked him, using her tongue to tease the sweet spot where head met shaft, he fired off another couple of snaps, close-ups of her mouth stretched widely around his considerable girth. Whether these were also for Max, or private snaps to keep and look at once they had gone their separate ways, so he could recall just how it had felt to be buried deep in her throat, she didn't know. It wasn't her place to question him on the matter. She just kept swirling her tongue over and around his cockhead, wishing her hands were free so she could stroke his balls and the sensitive seam between them, something she'd come to discover he particularly enjoyed.

Just before he came, he pulled out, so he could aim his come over her tightly bound body, as if he were marking her as his own. Again, he took photographs of the creamy liquid trickling over her skin, contrasted against the red of the rope, though his hands trembled so much she was sure the resulting shots would be blurry and out of focus.

When he released her, he held her close, running his fingers over the faint marks the ropes had left against her skin, telling her what a good girl she'd been and how much she had pleased him. And somehow, that washed away all the discomfort, all the embarrassment she felt at being tied and rendered a receptacle for his pleasure. Whatever he instructed her to do, however much pain he forced her to take, the rewards were always worth it.

She kept telling herself how lucky she'd been that Jason had bid for her, and not one of the other men. She'd seen Simone take such a public whipping, and the story had filtered back to her of the machine with the freakish built-in dildo which Adele had been made to ride. One afternoon, following her master through the corridors, she had come across one of the house girls being led the other way. The girl was on the end of a leash, with Mistress Delice urging her to hurry up. That wasn't such an unusual sight; Jessica knew all too well these girls were at the beck and call of whoever chose to use them, whether that was one of the unaccompanied men or the more senior members of Damon Barada's staff. What alarmed her was the faux horse's tail protruding from between the girl's bottom cheeks; from the angle at which it emerged, Jessica could guess all too well where whatever anchored that tail in place had been plugged.

Compared to those ordeals, having to display her pussy on command, or take a paddling in front of her husband, seemed like small beer. Those humiliations she could cope with, and she hoped Jason wouldn't decide to push her any further.

That evening, Jessica was sent to answer a knock at her master's door, only to discover Nathalie standing there. She wondered why the maid hadn't come waltzing straight into the room as she had before; she didn't suppose the threat of a punishment if she did was putting the girl off, not judging by her ecstatic reaction to the treatment she'd received at Jason's hands.

'*Bonsoir, madame*, I have the dress I was instructed to bring for you.' She held out a garment shrouded in one of the clear plastic covers Jessica was more used to seeing when she picked up her dry cleaning.

'Dress?' Jessica asked, taking it from Nathalie's hands.

'Yes, I've picked you out a special outfit for tonight,' Jason informed her. 'We're dining at Damon's table. Do you have the rest of the outfit, Nathalie?'

'Yes, *monsieur*, the shoes, the make-up and the –' Whatever she'd been about to add, she stopped, as if not wanting to spoil a secret.

'Very good. Jessica, I want you to go in the bathroom and change.' He placed her make-up bag on top of the dress. For the past few days she hadn't worn as much as a slick of lip gloss, and it felt strange to be given her war paint once more. 'Wear your hair up; I know Damon likes that in a woman. Everything else will be waiting for you out here when you're ready. And thank you, Nathalie, that will be all.'

By now, leaving the bathroom door open was second nature to her. She ran water into the basin, and washed her face and hands. The noises she could hear as she patted herself dry with the towel indicated that Jason was hunting for something in the bedroom closet. Was he dressing up too? She remembered him as she'd first seen him, in the suit that looked as though he'd borrowed it from someone a size smaller than himself, and suppressed a grin. No wonder he wanted her to impress Damon Barada; she doubted he'd be doing it himself.

The dress he'd picked out for her seemed, at first glance, fairly demure; floor length and with long, tight-fitting sleeves. But the moment she put it on, she realised it was anything but. The floaty chiffon, in a moss green shade that flattered her fair colouring, was sheer enough to reveal that she wore absolutely nothing beneath it. The peaks of her nipples pressed against the thin fabric, and when she moved it clung indecently to the slight rise of her pubic mound. Still, considering how much of the time she'd spent at the resort naked, this classed as a slight improvement.

At her master's instruction, she piled her hair up, pinning most of it in place while leaving a few tendrils to frame her face. She took time over her make-up, outlining her eyes in smoky shades, and applying two coats of rich brick-red lipstick. A small blob of clear gloss in the centre of her lower lip – a tip she'd picked up from one of the fashion magazines she read – gave her lips a wet, kissable appearance. She hadn't glammed up like this since the ill-fated trip to Envied which had set this whole bizarre chain of events in motion, and she hoped Jason would be pleased with the result.

The grin on his face as she re-entered the bedroom let her know how much he liked her outfit. Though she had to admit he looked surprisingly good himself: the dinner suit he'd put on, with its tuxedo jacket and dark, slim-fitting trousers, gave him an elegance she'd never suspected he might possess.

'Beautiful,' he murmured. 'Now all we need are the finishing touches.'

When she saw the shoes he expected her to wear, she almost gasped aloud. No stranger to fuck-me heels, if she'd seen these in a shop she would have rejected them as something designed exclusively for strippers. With thick platform soles in clear Lucite, and heels that must have been a good six inches high, walking in them would present a serious challenge. Still, she obediently slipped them on, and tried to accustom herself to their towering height.

'Now, one last thing,' her master said, moving to stand behind her. She couldn't see him fastening a piece of jewellery around her neck, but it wouldn't have surprised her if he'd produced a collar and leash; it seemed to be the traditional way of leading slave girls through the corridors here. What she hadn't expected was for him to catch hold of first one arm, then the other, and guide them into what felt like a thick latex sheath that compressed them together. When he allowed her to take a look at her reflection, she saw she was actually wearing some kinky version of an elbow-length opera glove.

'You look so good in bondage,' he told her, 'but I thought we'd try something more elegant for evening wear. Now, let's go. Dinner will be served shortly.'

She tottered out of the room after Jason, gradually becoming used to the feeling of walking in the stripper shoes. The thickness of the platforms helped to offset the height of the heels, and she began to understand how someone might be able to negotiate a dance routine around a pole in these things, though it wasn't anything she envisaged herself doing any time soon – unless it was to please her master, of course.

In the room that doubled as dining space and ballroom, one of the house girls showed them to their table. They were seated with Adele's husband, whose name Jessica learnt was Malcolm, and another of the single male guests, a gaunt, shaven-headed individual in a startling neon blue jacket who introduced himself only as Cyrus.

'He's a conceptual artist, whatever that might be,' Jason whispered in her ear once they'd sat down. 'All I know is he's famous enough not to need a surname, and rich enough to be able to spend his playtime here.'

Both men exchanged pleasantries with Jason while they waited for their host to arrive. Though they didn't openly acknowledge Jessica, the way their gazes studied her body, lingering on her breasts where they were visible beneath the sheer chiffon, made it clear they were all too aware of her presence. She felt all the men at the table, even the elderly and frail-looking Malcolm, would love to strip the dress from her and take a closer look at her charms. She looked round in search of Max, and saw him on a neighbouring table, sitting between Simone and the German pretty boy whose name still eluded her.

At that moment, Damon Barada joined them, taking the unoccupied seat next to Jessica. 'Gentlemen, good evening,' he said genially. 'And thank you, Jason, for bringing your very lovely slave girl for our amusement.'

Damon ran a hand down Jessica's cheek, and his grizzled face split in a grin. When his fingers moved lower, brushing over her shoulder blade, she began to suspect she might be his entertainment for the evening.

His arrival seemed to be the cue for dinner to be served. Half-dressed girls moved between the tables, bringing plates containing the starter course. Jessica found a plate of asparagus, dripping with butter, being placed in front of her. She stared at it in despair; with her hands bound in the glove, she couldn't pick up her cutlery. Surely her master didn't expect her to bend and put her face to the plate, as she did with her breakfast every morning. She couldn't cope with the humiliation, not with an audience and dressed in her finery.

'Allow me,' Damon said. He prodded an asparagus spear with his fork, and put it to her mouth. Instinctively, she seemed to know he wanted her to make a show of eating it, so she licked the butter from its length as sensuously as she could before biting into it. It tasted good, but she had to wait until Damon had cleared his plate before he let her have another piece.

This time, when he picked the asparagus up, he did so with his fingers. The butter ran down on to his hand, and Jessica licked it from his skin. She thought she heard a groan from the other side of the table as she did.

The final piece was almost dangled before her face, and when she bit at it, the butter trickled onto her chin. Damon wiped it up with his finger, which he pushed between her lips. Jessica suckled it, and as she did she felt a hand stroke her thigh through her dress. She knew it had to be Jason caressing her, but she kept her attention firmly on Damon, knowing he was her focus tonight. Though those men who owned slaves for the week appeared to rank higher in the resort's pecking order than those who were single, Barada was clearly the alpha male in the room, and she gave him the deference he was due.

While their empty plates were being cleared away, he grew bolder in his approach.

'So, Jason,' he said, slipping an arm around Jessica's shoulders, 'how are you enjoying your stay here?'

'Very much,' her master replied. 'When people told me this place was a dominant male's dream come true, I wasn't sure I believed them, but now – well, if anything, it's even better than they said.'

'And you're making the most of having a submissive beauty at your beck and call?' Almost as if unaware of what he was doing, Barada let his hand drop onto Jessica's breast. He brushed her nipple with the tip of his thumb. She glanced over to Jason, wondering how he was reacting to Barada's decision to exercise his *droit de seigneur* so openly. It was a foolish thing to worry about, she knew; hadn't she already been effectively handed over by Max to whoever might care to use her? But, deep down, she had come to think of herself as Jason's, at least until this bizarre week was over, and she could do nothing without his permission. When he gave the subtlest nod of acknowledgement, she knew he was enjoying the thought of what might be about to happen.

'Of course.' Jason replied to the question Jessica had almost forgotten Barada had asked. 'You've already seen what she can do with her mouth. And she's just as talented with her fingers, believe me.'

'Really? I must bear that in mind, though it's pretty hard for her to do anything with them in those gloves, hey?' Damon reached his hand into the neckline of her dress, and caressed her bare breast. She knew the other diners at the table would be able to see the precise movements of his fingers through the diaphanous fabric.

Even when the waitress arrived with their main course – fillets of a meaty white fish she didn't recognise, served with lightly steamed vegetables and spiced rice – he didn't stop fondling her. He forked fish and rice into his mouth with one hand, while the other continued to cup and squeeze her breasts. From time to time, he fed her from her own plate, while Jason, Malcolm, and Cyrus chatted among themselves and tucked into their food as if nothing out of the ordinary were happening. All the while, the waitresses kept circulating, topping up the glasses of the guests. Even Jessica was allowed a few sips of wine, with her master putting the glass to her lips so she could drink.

At last, Damon pushed his plate away. 'D'you want to know a secret?' he said. 'The fish we've just eaten – that was a 70-pound blue marlin, and I caught it myself this morning. It fought like hell, but I reeled it in eventually.'

'It was delicious,' Malcolm commented, 'but then there's nothing like really fresh fish.'

'And sea fishing's the best exercise there is,' Damon replied. 'Really builds up the biceps. Just what you need if you know you're going to be spanking a naughty girl's ass.'

While they waited for their dessert, Damon changed his mode of attack. Having groped Jessica's breasts till her nipples were ripe and aching, he scooped each heavy globe from out of the dress's neckline in turn, and left them there, proudly bare. As shameful as his casual exposure of her body might be, Jessica shivered with the thrill of knowing her tits were now the focus of all four men seated round the table. If Max were to glance over now, he would see exactly what Damon had done to her, and know that she had submitted willingly to the desires of their host.

Damon slipped his hand beneath the crisp white tablecloth, so he could massage her pussy through her dress. He pushed the thin chiffon between her pouting lips, wetting the fabric in the juices that gathered there. His grin was wolfish, the tracery of lines around his eyes deepening. He could tell just how much being played with so publicly was turning her on.

'I could have you coming in front of every man here, just like that –' His fingertip brushed over her clit, even that light, casual touch causing her to writhe in her seat with frustrated longing. 'Max should have brought you here so much sooner. The fun we've missed out on …'

Jessica whimpered, fighting to retain a measure of

control. 'Please,' she said, 'I'm not allowed to come without my master's permission.'

'And would he punish you if you did?'

'I'm sure he would,' she replied, knowing her words were giving Damon all the encouragement he needed to keep stroking her so intimately.

'Your dessert, sir.'

The words distracted Damon from his explorations, as the waitress set down a small metal stand in the centre of the table. She carefully balanced a flame-red ceramic pot on the stand, before lighting a flame beneath the contraption.

'Ah, chocolate fondue. My favourite,' Damon said with obvious pleasure.

Beside the fondue pot, the waitress placed a tray, laden with pieces of fruit – chunks of banana, whole strawberries, slices of kiwi and star fruit – as well as mini marshmallows and bite-size pieces of sponge cake, all designed to be dipped into the rich, gooey chocolate mixture.

'Do dig in, please, gentlemen,' Damon instructed, once the waitress had moved on to perform the same ritual at the next table. He picked up one of the long-handled, two-pronged forks provided, and speared a piece of banana, which he dipped into the fondue before popping the confection into his mouth. Repeating the action with a strawberry, he offered the fruit to Jessica. He took no more care than he had with the asparagus, and chocolate – hot, but not painfully so – dripped onto her right breast. Whether he'd planned that to happen or not she wasn't entirely sure, but as she chewed on the proffered strawberry, Damon bent to lick the traces of fondue from her skin.

He helped himself to a couple more pieces of fruit, then a marshmallow. Jessica sat patiently watching. The men were joking among themselves as they dipped their forks in the fondue. A roar went up from one of the other tables, and Jessica turned her head to see what might be the cause of the commotion. Adele had risen to her feet, and Simone's husband had pushed back his chair and was patting his lap as he waited for her to climb onto it.

'In Switzerland, it's traditional for the diner to pay some kind of forfeit if whatever they're dipping in the fondue falls from the fork and can't be retrieved,' Damon explained. 'Here, it's the table slave who pays.'

Hearing that, Jessica sucked in a breath. Would the other diners at her table let their titbits of food drop into the pot on purpose, in the hope of spanking her? Would she find herself being pulled over Cyrus's knee, or old Malcolm's, and receiving a half-dozen hard swats to her naked rump, just like Simone was getting now? Part of her hoped desperately that wouldn't happen, even as the rest of her hoped it would.

But the two men seemed more interested in the show Damon was putting on for them, feeding Jessica in a deliberately messy fashion, so that more of each forkful went on her tits than in her mouth and had to be licked from her skin. Soon, her master had joined in the fun; as he suckled on one nipple and Damon on the other, all pretence that this had ever been about food dispensed with, Jessica writhed against the seat and silently begged for permission to come.

Damon had set down his fork, and now his hand was at her pussy again, pushing the saturated fabric up into her hole, each movement causing the chiffon to brush against her clit and give her almost, but not quite enough stimulation to push her into a forbidden orgasm. It would, she knew, only take a very little more of this treatment and she would be screaming out her pleasure to the whole room, every eye on her as she came around Barada's thick, probing fingers. The punishment that followed such an indiscretion would no doubt be quite spectacular, but she didn't care, just as long as her master would say the words she longed to hear ...

'Are you finished, sir?' The waitress' voice broke the erotic spell. Jason sat upright, pulling away from Jessica, and Damon let her nipple slip from his lips to answer the girl.

'Yes, you can take everything away and bring us coffee when you're ready.'

That seemed to be the cue for the conversation to return to more mundane matters.

'Do you mind if I slip out for a cigarette?' Cyrus asked, reaching into his pocket to pull out a silver cigarette case bearing a monogrammed "C".

Barada shook his head. 'Not at all. But hurry back soon. That little redhead slut who served us dessert doesn't think I saw her spill a couple of strawberries on the floor as she cleared the plates away, but I did, and I'm going to make damn sure she gets the appropriate punishment.'

'Well, before the fun begins, I need some air,' Jason said. 'Come with me, Jessica.'

He pulled out her chair, leaving his jacket, which he'd removed at some point between their main course and dessert, draped over the back of his own, and guided her to her feet. Obediently, Jessica trotted after him as he left the room, not even turning her head to see whether Max had noticed them go. They stepped out to join Cyrus on the veranda, where he stood leaning on the balustrade, staring out at the ocean. The moon hung low and full in the sky, casting its cold light over the gently rippling waves.

Noticing them standing close by, Cyrus took a reflective drag on his cigarette and nodded to them. 'You think this view is something,' he said. 'Well, you should see the way the pool looks tonight.'

'Pool?' Jessica couldn't help asking, even though she knew her master would chastise her later for speaking out of turn.

'D'you want to see it?' Jason asked. When she nodded, he commanded, 'Follow me, then.'

He took her down a short flight of steps that led off the side of the veranda, and across a stretch of marble tiling that led to the resort's spa area – something she should have guessed a complex such as this would possess.

If this had been the kind of holiday she'd hoped for when Max had first told her he was bringing her to Isla Barada, she knew she'd have spent plenty of her time here. Back in London, she enjoyed nothing more than a girly spa day with her friends, being massaged and pampered and swapping gossip over a cocktail in the bar afterwards. She wondered if she would ever feel able to tell those friends about all the depraved things that had been done to her during the last few days, and how much she had enjoyed being used and abused by Barada's wealthy guests.

The waters of the hot tub were silent at the moment, waiting for someone to press the button and send them churning into life. How tempting it would be to slip into that tub, and let the bubbling jets massage her skin. If she sat in just the right position, she'd be able to direct those jets right onto her clit, and reawaken the delicious feelings that had been cut short when the waitress had interrupted their kinky little scene.

With some difficulty, she dragged her mind away from her own need for gratification, and continued her contemplation of the spa facilities. The infinity pool was the real centrepiece. It must, she thought, have cost Damon Barada a fortune to have its foundations cut into the hillside, so that as swimmers approached the far edge, they received the impression that the water was about to tumble into nothingness, the lip of the pool merging seamlessly with the horizon. With darkness fallen and the moon so bright in the sky, the view might have been diminished, but spotlights built into the pool's blue-tiled walls revealed the full glory of its other asset – the mosaic relief on its bottom. Mimicking the designs of Ancient Rome, it depicted mermaids frolicking with what appeared to be Neptune, the god of the sea.

Taking a couple of steps nearer to the edge of the pool, Jessica took a closer look at the design. Of course it had been given Damon's signature erotic twist, and Neptune appeared to be quite enjoying the attention of his bare-breasted companions, given by the size of the erection that jutted out from the folds of his robe.

'Come on, Jessica,' Jason said from somewhere behind her, 'we're going back for coffee now.'

'Yes, sir.' She knew she should follow him at once,

but she couldn't resist taking one last, slow look around. After all, there was no chance of her coming back here before the end of her stay, and she had to imprint the beauty of the night sky and the gently rippling waters of the pool on her memory.

'Hurry up, girl, don't dawdle!'

Jessica turned sharply at the sound of her master's command, only for the heel of her shoe to snap right off. She lost her balance, toppling backwards into the pool. Her mouth and nose filled with chlorinated water, and panic overtook her. Jessica had never been the strongest of swimmers and now, with her hands fastened behind her in a bondage glove that was impossible for her to remove unaided, she sank like a stone towards the bottom of the pool. Not wanting her last sight on earth to be the tiled outline of Neptune's grotesquely huge cock, she kicked off her shoes and did her best to push upwards, managing to break the surface briefly and scream for help, for her master, for Max.

Then she was sinking again, struggling in the folds of wet chiffon that hampered the movement of her legs. Closing her eyes tight, certain this was the end, she uttered a silent prayer. Then something cleaved the water with a heavy splash. Strong arms wrapped themselves around her from behind, and she was being hauled up, and towards the steps at the shallow end of the pool.

'Hey, take it easy, Jessica,' Jason's voice murmured, as he worked to unbuckle the bondage glove with one hand while holding her steady with the other. Once he had worked it down and off her arms, he tossed it onto the tiled lip of the pool, then helped her up the steps and out to safety. Still clinging to him, she coughed up a little water, feeling sick and disorientated, but all too conscious of how much worse things might have been without her master's intervention.

'Thank you,' she murmured, looking up into his concerned face. He'd taken off his shoes before diving in to rescue her, but even in his stockinged feet he still towered over her. His sodden shirt was plastered to his broad chest, and droplets of water dripped from his hair. Yet – and maybe she was just viewing him as her white knight, her rescuer in her hour of need – she thought she'd never seen Jason look as good as he did at that moment.

'What kind of master would I be if my girl was in danger of drowning and I didn't do anything to help her?' he said. His hand smoothed over the bare skin of her back. 'Now, come on, let's get you dry.'

He unzipped the dress and pushed it down off her shoulders, letting the saturated garment slither to the floor. Jessica stepped out of it, for once feeling no shame at being naked before him, even though he was still fully dressed. Piles of clean, fluffy towels stood in a wooden rack by the wall. Jason took one and wrapped it round Jessica's body. He used another to fashion a turban for her hair. Then he picked up the wet evening dress and made to lead her out of the spa area.

'My shoes –' she began.

'Don't worry, I'll arrange for someone to collect them for you.'

Her small hand enveloped in his big one, they walked down the corridor, past the ballroom. Jessica could hear music and raised voices coming from behind the closed doors, the party still continuing without them, but she had no desire to step inside and witness whatever depraved scenes might be taking place within, not even to retrieve her master's jacket, which still hung on the back of his chair. How on earth would she explain why Jason was soaked to the skin, why she was swaddled in towels from the spa? No, best leave them to it, and she would take whatever punishment she deserved for her act of flagrant disobedience; it was all she deserved.

Chapter Fourteen

Once in Jason's room, she was ordered to sit on the bed. She waited while he went into the bathroom to strip off and towel himself down, thanking her stars that his key card had still worked, even though it had been in his trouser pocket when he'd dived into the pool. If it hadn't, would he have sent her down to reception to beg for a replacement, or would he have taken her back to the room she shared with Honey, and forced her to sleep chained to her bed?

When he returned, the towel was wrapped round his waist and his dark hair stood up in damp little spikes. Despite all she'd gone through, her pussy fluttered with unexpected lust at the sight of him.

Sitting on the bed beside her, Jason removed her towel turban, pushing the wet strands of hair away from her face as they tumbled down. She trembled at his touch, though he seemed to misinterpret the reason.

'You've had a shock, Jess,' he told her. 'I'll get you a glass of brandy.' Before she could protest, he sprang up from the bed and went over to the minibar, busying himself in fixing them both a drink.

'Master.' He looked round at the sound of her voice, squatting on his haunches with the bottle of Armagnac in one hand. Had he given her permission to speak? Would she be punished for her impertinence? Not worrying about any demerit marks she might be racking up, she ploughed on. 'Why are you being so nice to me?'

'Nice?' Jason looked genuinely baffled.

'Well, some of the other masters here, they'd have saved me from drowning, but they'd have made me towel them dry afterwards, not the other way round. And they certainly wouldn't have let me have a drink to calm my nerves.'

He came back to the bed, pressing a brandy glass into her hand and taking a sip from his own before answering her. 'Some of the guys here, they get so far into the fantasy, I think they forget there's a real woman on the end of their whip strokes. When all the bets are off and the usual rules don't apply, you behave in a way you might not do otherwise. You know, I don't honestly know whether all of them actually like the woman they bought. But I do know that I like you, Jessica. And I like Max, and I want him to have the submissive he's dreamt of by the end of the week. And that means using plenty of carrot, as well as stick.'

Jason grinned, his face lighting up. Jessica caught herself thinking again what beautiful eyes he had, then reminded herself sharply of the real truth behind his words. This week was all about teaching her to submit for Max's benefit, not that of the man who sat beside her now.

That didn't stop her swallowing a big gulp of brandy, surrendering to its fiery warmth. Already, the terrifying sensations of being dragged down to the bottom of the swimming pool, unable to free herself from her bonds, were beginning to seem like nothing more than a bad dream.

'Master, you remember you said that talking about our personal lives wasn't important. Well – I think it is. I think it'll help me serve you better – and Max – if I know more about you.'

Jason considered her words for a moment. 'OK, I'll tell you whatever you want to know, but in return you've got to answer any questions I might have. Absolute honesty on both sides, right?'

'Of course.' Jessica paused, though the only question she felt she really needed an answer to was the one that had nagged at her since the moment Jason had bought her. 'In that case, tell me how you come to be among Damon Barada's circle of dominants. I mean, Honey's husband's a London property tycoon, Wesley Cole designs best-selling computer games, Max manufactures eco-friendly lighting ... So how did you make your millions?'

Just for a moment, he looked embarrassed. 'Absolute honesty, right? Me and my big mouth. Well, the truth is I haven't made millions, and I don't think I ever will. I work as a personal trainer, and my stay here is being paid for by a grateful client. Otherwise, I'd never have been able to afford it.'

'But surely you must have some money?' Jessica persisted. 'Look at how much you paid for me.'

'That was your husband's money, not mine,' Jason confessed. 'He wanted to make sure Sebastian Voller didn't buy you'

'Voller,' Jessica repeated, and something else that had evaded her till now became clear. 'He's the German guy who was sitting with Max at dinner, isn't he? Now I know where I knew him from – he and Max were once bidding for the same contract, and Sebastian Voller won it. They're not exactly friends, from what I recall.'

'Yes, and Voller isn't exactly the kind of man you need to initiate you into submission, believe me. Max wanted you kept away from the guy, because he was frightened of how he would treat you if he got his hands on you. And I was just the person he used to prevent that from happening. I'm sorry if that's not what you wanted to hear, Jessica, but it's the truth.'

All her suspicions had been confirmed. Jason didn't belong here, not really. And to hear that Max, of all people, had subbed him her auction price ...

Almost as if he'd read her mind, Jason asked, 'So tell me, Jessica, does that mean I'm not worthy to be your master?'

She considered the question, amazed to discover the first thing that sprang to her mind was Honey's assertion that money mattered more than love. Max had only done what he'd done because he loved her, she knew that. He wanted her to be safe, to be treated with consideration for her own needs, as well as those of the man who mastered her. And Jason had no money, but that didn't matter, not when he could take her places she'd never been, with his commanding words and the flat of his hand and his big, beautiful cock ... 'No, master. The question is whether I'm worthy to be your slave.'

'Never doubt that, Jessica.'

Their faces were only inches apart, Jessica's lips slightly parted as she stared into Jason's devastatingly blue eyes. The line between them was clear – master and submissive, trainer and initiate – and she knew she was in danger of breaching it. Some things, once done, could not be undone. Yet, not caring about the consequences, she gave in to the instinct that overrode all good sense, and pressed her mouth to Jason's in a soft kiss. His eyes widened, then he pulled her close, the kiss deepening as his tongue pushed between her lips. Her hands cupped the point of his chin, stubble prickling her skin. When they finally broke apart, breathless, she somehow found the voice to say, 'I'm sorry, I shouldn't have –'

She'd kissed so many men, revelling in the feel of their lips, their tongues, their obvious need for her, but with Jason she'd experienced something she usually felt with Max alone – the knowledge that this was right, that she wanted to do it again. And despite her stammered apology, her body ached with the need to be in Jason's arms, to kiss him till her mouth was swollen and bruised.

'Hey, it's OK.' Jason traced the backs of his fingers over the contours of her cheek. 'You had a terrible shock, and I'm the one who should be sorry. Leaving you unsupervised when you were so close to the side of that pool, with your hands bound and in those stupid heels ... It was just asking for trouble.'

She couldn't believe he was apologising to her. If she hadn't disobeyed his order and returned to his side as soon as he'd called her, none of this would have happened. Prostrating herself before him, she murmured, 'Master, I don't think I'll ever be worthy of you.'

'Don't talk like that.' He pulled her up to face him, though she struggled to meet his gaze. 'You're doing so well, Jessica. I'm sure lots of women would have turned round and got straight back on the boat as soon as they realised what kind of place Isla Barada really is, but you – you've done everything Max has asked of you, everything I've asked of you. And tonight, in that dress, letting Damon do whatever he wanted to you – God, you looked magnificent. If you were mine …'

He let the sentence trail off, as if aware that he, just like Jessica, was in imminent danger of crossing a line. Then his mouth was on hers again, and his kiss told her everything his words dared not; how much he wanted her, how it could be if he was her permanent master, rather than merely the man whose job was to train her for her husband's pleasure.

Her fingers twined in Jason's hair, still damp from his rescue act; the sour chlorine scent of the pool still lingered faintly on his skin, but his own male aroma was strongest in her nostrils, exciting her on a base, primitive level. His kisses left a wet trail down her neck, as he nipped at the skin with his teeth. She wanted those little sucking bites to mark her, to leave the evidence of his presence on her body.

Their limbs tangled together as he lowered her back onto the bed. Through the towel, the hot, hard bar of his erection thrust at her, and she rubbed herself against it, her juices soaking the soft terry cloth. He could take her now; she was ready. In truth, she'd been ready from the moment she'd walked out of the bedroom to find him standing in his tuxedo, confident and elegant in a way she'd never imagined he could be. She'd been proud to walk into the ballroom, bound by him – bound to him in ways she could never have expected. Who cared if Max had manipulated the situation for his own ends? It had brought her to this point, where she was on the verge of surrendering herself utterly to Jason, and right now that was all that mattered.

Her master's mouth moved lower, latching on to her nipple once more. Again he bit at her flesh, worrying the tight bud between his teeth, and all the while she moaned and begged for more. Jessica tugged at the knot in his towel, pulling it open so they lay, skin to skin, with nothing to impede her from feeling every inch of his broad, muscular body against her own.

Jason's tongue snaked down her cleavage, laving her skin and coming to rest in the well of her navel. The hot, sinuous tongue-tip tickled her there, and she giggled and writhed against him.

'Oh, you like that, do you?' he asked, raising his head to look her in the eye.

'I like everything you do to me,' she admitted.

'Even the things that hurt?'

'Especially the things that hurt.' She'd never thought she'd ever find herself making such a confession, but Jason didn't seem fazed. He simply kept kissing her, still making his inexorable way down over the swell of her belly towards her wet, waiting pussy.

She kept expecting him to pull away at any moment. Oral sex was something a master received, not gave; the expression of a slave's submission – or so she'd come to believe. Jason, though, appeared to have ideas of his own on the subject. With firm hands, he parted her legs wide, and took a moment to stare at the treasures the movement revealed. Jessica almost blushed; she'd never been the subject of such intense, almost loving scrutiny, not even from Max. But he seemed to like what he saw well enough; he reached out a finger, brushing it over the intricate folds.

'I once read that a woman's cunt is like an oyster, hiding a pearl at its heart,' he said. 'A precious, beautiful pearl ...' As he spoke, he touched her clit so lightly she thought she'd imagined it, but in combination with his reverent words, the stimulation was enough to have her groaning low in her throat and pushing herself towards him for more of the same.

Taking hold of her thighs, Jason made himself comfortable between them, easing her legs over his shoulders so that her crotch was right up against his face. The stubble on his chin pricked at the insides of her thighs and she knew if he planned to settle in there for a while he'd leave the sensitive skin irritated and sore, but she'd already accepted that a little pain was a price more than worth paying for the pleasure he was capable of giving her.

His mouth engulfed her pussy, and she knew at once this was a man who enjoyed the act of licking a woman. His tongue swept along the whole length of her cleft, right down to the crinkled bud of her arsehole, and he sucked her soft inner labia right into his mouth, making smacking noises with his lips as though he relished the taste of her. With her bum cheeks gripped securely in his big hands, he could hold her in place for as long as he wished to feast on her, and Jessica lay back, consumed by the intense sensations coursing through her body. She watched him eat her, his expression rapt, and knew that after tonight she could never go back to the meaningless one-night stands she'd used as a way of distracting herself from her dwindling sex life with Max. They'd been fun, and she'd loved the power she'd wielded over those young studs with their pretty faces and firm bodies, but none of them had ever made her feel the way Jason did now; the way Max could make her feel, if the two of them were prepared to work on their marriage, and take it back to how it had been in the early days.

Jason's tongue returned to its squirming exploration of her rear hole, driving all thoughts of Max from Jessica's mind. She'd never been so thoroughly licked here, and she wasn't quite sure she should be enjoying it as much as she was. But when Jason slipped a finger into her channel, while still lapping at her arse, she could no longer worry about whether this was right and proper.

He broke off from his oral ministrations long enough to murmur, 'Come for me, Jessica. Come in my mouth, my gorgeous slut.'

As if those words had pressed a button somewhere deep inside her, Jessica's orgasm hit her with surprising force. The stars danced behind her closed eyelids, as bright as those in the night sky outside, and she yelled out, 'Oh yes, Jason, yes!'

He licked her through the hard, heaving waves of her climax, and the shallow ripples that followed it, and at last he lowered her gently to the mattress. While she fought to recover something of her equilibrium, Jason slipped off the bed and went to find a condom, his rigid cock seeming to lead the way. When he returned and made to open the packet, she snatched it from his fingers. 'Allow me,' she said.

She'd learned the trick a long time ago, as a way of impressing Max; now she wanted to do it to return the compliment Jason had just paid her with his oral skills. Encouraging him to sit on the edge of the bed, she got down on her knees before him and popped the condom into her mouth. Jason said nothing, simply waited with bated breath as Jessica took hold of his cock and slowly, carefully, rolled the sheath over his length using her tongue and lips. Once she'd swallowed as much of him as she was able, she finished the job with her fingers, covering him all the way to the base of his shaft.

'Don't let Damon know you can do that,' Jason told her. 'He'll want to keep you here as one of his house girls.'

'Oh, I think Max would have something to say if he tried that,' she replied.

'Yeah, and so would I. God, Jessica, I really need to fuck you.'

He reached for her, and they rolled over on the bed together. Jessica pushed him down on his back, and straddled his groin in one fluid movement. His cock stood up proudly, almost demanding that she sink down onto it, but she teased him for a moment, gyrating so her pussy lips brushed over his latex-covered helmet, but making no more contact than that.

'Damn it, Jessica, stop tormenting me or I'll spank you so hard you won't be able to sit down for a day!'

'Is that a threat or a promise?' She grinned down at him, repeating the motion and frustrating him further.

'Do as you're told, you minx,' he ordered, reaching round to give her arse a sharp, ringing slap.

Aware there was plenty more where that had come from, Jessica lowered her pussy slowly onto his length, sighing with pleasure as the thick meat spread her wide. Inch by inch, she took him inside her, until she was full of hot, gently pulsing man-flesh. The look of pure lust on Jason's face let her know he was savouring the sensation every bit as much as she was.

For a moment, she didn't move; just gave her inner muscles a little flex that had him groaning. From the open window, noises rose up from the beach – male laughter and a soft female squeal that contained much more lust than pain. Jessica ignored them, her whole attention on the man whose cock fitted so snugly inside her, and who lay patiently, waiting for her to ride him. She couldn't deny him a moment longer, and she began to rock back and forth on him, her movements slow and undulating.

'Oh yes,' he murmured, as she squeezed his cock again. He half rose, and she leant forward, their mouths meeting in a tongue-twining kiss. Jason reached round to grasp her bum cheeks, and now he was sitting up too, his cock buried in her at a deeper angle, reaching parts of her that brought a gasp to her lips and triggered a fierce desire to come once more. As their passion mounted, she moved faster, Jason's strength and flexibility allowing her to adopt more athletic positions than she normally managed with Max. She couldn't get enough of it, of him. The scent of him, raw and earthy, inflamed her senses; sweat shone on his chest. Her fingernails raked at his back as he began to thrust up into her, moving in a rhythm that matched hers as he grew closer to his own climax.

'Need to come,' he grunted. 'Need you to come with me.'

His cock jerked, and his grip on her buttocks grew tighter, holding her still as he came. The knowledge that his spunk was flooding into the condom, and the intense connection she felt to him, sparked another orgasm in Jessica. She clung to him, racked by convulsions that robbed her of speech, of rational thought.

It could only have been moments before he eased himself from her body and went to dispose of the condom, but time had lost its meaning. The groans and cries of the couple on the beach intruded briefly into her thoughts. She had no idea who might be fucking out there, but she hoped they were having as good a time as she and Jason just had.

When he returned from the bathroom, he made no move to reach for the chains that usually tethered her to his bed. Instead, he pulled the covers over the two of them, and they fell asleep in each other's arms.

Chapter Fifteen

Jason could still taste the sweetness of Jessica's lips on his own. He stared at himself in the bathroom mirror, unable to believe he'd done such a crazy thing last night. He shouldn't have responded when she'd kissed him, shouldn't have claimed her mouth, even though it had been there for the taking, shouldn't have fucked her with all the passion he possessed, shouldn't have slept with her curled up in his arms. But everything about the woman drove him to distraction, and he could no longer pretend to be only the dispassionate master, leading her along the path to submission.

This was all so fucked up. It had started as the most exciting game of his life – taking an inexperienced woman and teaching her to obey his every command – but somehow it had evolved into something much more serious. And he couldn't allow himself to have any kind of real emotional feelings for her, not when she was another man's wife. After all, it wasn't as though he was taming her for his own benefit.

If circumstances had been different – if she'd been married to that self-satisfied bastard Voller, or an old fool like Malcolm Quinn, who only wanted a flesh-and-blood Barbie doll to hang off his arm – he'd have had no qualms about letting his feelings for Jessica deepen. But the worst part of all this was that he really liked Max Sheringham, and he didn't want to do anything which might damage the couple's marriage.

But it really wasn't like him to fall for someone so fast. He'd experienced lust at first sight any number of times – and his initial reaction when Jessica had been brought to the auction block that night, half-dressed and in restraint, embodying every horny MILF fantasy he'd ever had, had been purely physical. If he hadn't been so attracted to her, he'd have kept silent when Damon asked for someone to start the bidding, and spent the week letting the house girls attend to his needs. He wouldn't have been sucked into the bitter battle of wills between Max and Voller, and he'd have gone back to London with enough happy memories of this week in paradise to last a lifetime. But now lust threatened to turn into something deeper, and he couldn't afford to let that happen.

In his bed, Jessica still slept. The maid would be here any moment now, and he supposed he ought to wake her and shackle her in place before that happened; he wasn't sure of the etiquette in these situations, but he felt he needed to make sure it was still obvious they were master and slave. But somehow he just couldn't bear to wake her.

His mind flashed back to Jessica as she'd been in his arms the night before, so open and soft and vulnerable. Everything he wanted in a submissive, in a lover …

'Good morning, sir!' a voice called from the other room. Jason splashed cold water on his face, grabbed a towel, and emerged from the bathroom. The maid's interested gaze, hovering somewhere around his groin, reminded him that he hadn't bothered to pull his shorts on. Let her look; she'd probably seen every other man on the island naked, and been fucked by most of them too, most likely.

Jessica had woken at the girl's entrance, and was sitting up with the bedsheets pulled around her body. The maid said nothing; Jason suspected the girl simply assumed Jessica must be chained to the bed, as always, and had taken advantage of his absence from the room to sneak a little in the way of comfort.

'Jessica, did I tell you that you could get under the covers?' he snapped. He hoped the maid didn't see the quick little wink he aimed in Jessica's direction, letting her know his wrath was feigned for the benefit of the newcomer.

'I'm sorry, sir,' Jessica replied. She started to push the sheets aside, but Jason stepped in before she could reveal the lack of a cuff around her ankle.

He took the breakfast tray from the maid. 'I'd invite you to stay and watch her punishment,' he said, 'but I'd hate to keep anyone waiting for their breakfast. Don't worry, I'll make her display her stripes to you the next time she sees you – she hates having to do that.'

'Of course, sir. Enjoy your breakfast, sir.' The girl retreated from the room.'

'Wow, that was close,' Jason said. 'I didn't want her reporting back to anyone that I'd given you the privilege of sleeping in the bed. Might cause a riot among Honey and the others.'

'And you wouldn't want to be on the end of Honey's anger, now would you?' Jessica grinned.

'Oh, I could deal with her, don't you worry about that. But I'd far rather have the job of making sure you behave yourself. Which you're not, may I remind you?' He clicked his fingers. 'Get on the floor, Jessica, if you want any breakfast.'

His words, and the firmness with which they were delivered, re-established the boundaries between them instantly. Last night had been a delicious one-off; a shared moment when he'd allowed himself to fantasise that they might become something other than purely dominant and submissive. The truth was he only had a couple more days to train Jessica to do his – and Max's – bidding. After that, they would go their separate ways, and nothing he could do would alter that.

'I have something very special lined up for you today, Jessica.'

She had just emerged from the bathroom, freshly showered, swathed in a towel and with her wet hair fastened in a loose ponytail at the nape of her neck. While she'd been in the shower, one of the maids had paid a visit to the room, bringing her outfit for the day.

It should have stopped surprising her well before now that every outfit she was expected to wear was designed to make her appear slutty and available, but this one outdid all the rest. Lying on the bed was a babydoll nightie in diaphanous black nylon, along with a pair of matching panties so tiny they barely qualified as an item of clothing. White stockings completed the ensemble. She couldn't see any shoes, which suited her just fine, given the previous evening's footwear malfunction and its consequences. Perhaps it meant they wouldn't be leaving the room today. God knew she'd given Jason enough reasons to discipline her over the last 12 hours, not to mention all the little things she'd done which appeared to have gone unpunished so far.

When she picked up the clothes, in order to take them into the bathroom and change, her master shook his head. 'There's no time for that.'

She dropped the towel, aware of Jason's hungry gaze on her body. He'd seen her naked on enough occasions that it should no longer be of any special interest to him – but, she remembered, he only had a couple more days to enjoy the sight. Presumably he had to make the most of it while he had the chance.

The nightie, when she put it on, felt cheap against her skin – the kind of thing that could be picked up for a couple of pounds in any market back in London – and barely concealed the outline of her jutting nipples. The panties had stiff, scratchy lace around the leg holes, and the thin, elasticated waistband felt as though it would snap with one swift tug. Already she was gaining the impression that this outfit was designed to rip as it was removed, a thought that shouldn't have excited her, but did. She pulled on the stockings, which came halfway up her thighs and were held in place by thick, tightly gripping elastic, and she was ready.

Or at least, she thought she was. 'Just one last thing,' Jason said, and produced a thick black scarf from behind his back. He folded it in half along its length, and wrapped it around Jessica's head, tying it in place with a tight knot and effectively blindfolding her.

'Right, now let's go.'

'Go? Go where?' Jessica tried to keep the note of

panic out of her voice. The last thing she'd expected was to be deprived of her sight, and now he wanted her to leave the room.

'Come on, you'll be OK.' He took hold of her hand and led her towards the door. She heard it open, and took a couple of steps out into the corridor. The lock clicked shut behind her, and Jason began to guide her in the direction he wanted her to go.

Deprived of her sight, she found her other senses becoming keener to compensate. The carpet felt thick and soft beneath her stockinged feet, and she caught the scent of hibiscus on the air. Obediently, she followed her master along the corridor, but they couldn't have walked more than a few yards before he brought her to a halt and knocked on a door. So they must have come to the suite that neighboured Jason's on the right. But who did it belong to? Not Max, she was sure of that, and after everything Jason had said last night about Sebastian Voller, she couldn't believe he'd be delivering her to that man. Which left plenty of other candidates, but ...

The door opened. 'I've brought her,' Jason said.

She strained her ears, but whoever had answered the door made no response. None the wiser, Jessica found herself being ushered inside. Here, the air smelled of exotic spices and musk; it reminded her of a cologne she'd smelled at dinner last night, but who had been wearing it? Damon Barada? Malcolm Quinn? Cyrus, the man too famous to need a surname?

Jason's next words did nothing to enlighten her. She'd expected that once he'd brought her to this stranger, he would withdraw. Instead, he said, 'I've been very impressed with your progress over the week,

Jessica, but there are others who are keen to see how obedient you really are. So we've arranged this little gathering, and you're going to show everyone here what you can do, and just how good you are at following instructions.'

Everyone? So there was more than one person here besides the suite's registered occupant? And in that case, how many more? Two? Three? Every man on the island? And, most importantly, was any of them Max? 'Of course, master, but who is everyone?'

'Now, Jessica, that's really not a question you should be asking. You see, a good submissive must be willing and able to pleasure whoever her master requires, but it's in the nature of all of us to sometimes be a little squeamish where a potential partner is concerned. We might think they're too old for us, or too overweight, or too ugly, and we might hurt the feelings of that person by expressing that view, even if we phrase a refusal nicely. So today is all about learning to look beyond the surface – and the best way to do that is by not being able to see the surface in the first place. Hence the blindfold.'

She wasn't sure his logic would hold up if examined too closely, and she suspected he simply liked the way she looked with the scarf tied round her eyes, and the fact it rendered her almost helpless. But Jason continued outlining the event he had planned for her.

'So, in this room are a number of men. I'm not going to tell you who they are, or how many, and the point of this exercise isn't for you to try to guess. You're simply here to give pleasure to all of us, in whichever way we require it.'

So at least he was going to be part of this, she

reassured herself, even as the names and faces of the other male guests flashed through her mind. Some of them, she realised, she didn't actually know. But she couldn't think of anyone who was so physically repulsive she might draw the line at letting them touch her. She just had to trust that Jason wouldn't let her fall into the clutches of anyone who might do her harm, as he'd suggested Voller would – and though he hadn't said as much, allowing him to bring her into this suite had been all about trust.

'One more thing,' Jason added. 'No one apart from me will speak to you at any point. So they may find ... other ways of letting you know what they want. Now, gentleman, shall we begin?'

Jessica gasped as someone took hold of her from behind. She was pulled backwards, her bottom coming to rest against an unknown groin. A cool metal belt buckle bumped against the small of her back; the hard length of an erection sought to lodge itself between her cheeks. How long had these men been waiting here, she wondered, letting their anticipation, their horniness build with thoughts of having her under their control, blindfolded and vulnerable?

While the first man held her in place, a second began to explore the front of her body. He grasped her breasts, pushing them together as he caressed them in hard, circular motions. This was the cologne wearer; she could smell that arousing blend of spices on his skin as he pressed close to her, and despite Jason's instructions to forget about the possible identities of the men here, she couldn't help trying to work out who this was. Not Malcolm; she'd seen his hands at the dinner table, and they were bony, liver-spotted things, not the big paws that worked on her tits with such assurance. A sharp pinch of her nipple halted her guessing game, as she let out a little surprised mew. The pinch was repeated, more cruelly than the first time, yet the sensation that stabbed down from her tormented bud to her clit mingled pain with pleasure.

One of the hands that held her by the hips was removed, and she heard the clunk of the heavy buckle being unfastened, and the rapid grating of a zip being pulled down. Whoever was behind her clearly didn't bother with underwear, as, when he guided her back against his crotch, she could feel his bare cock, thick and hot, through the skimpy nylon of her nightdress.

Somewhere to her right, she swore she could hear whispering, though the voice was pitched too low for her to make out the words. Whoever it was had obviously been speaking to her master, for he now spoke up. 'Gentlemen, I've had a request to see more.'

In response, Cologne Man, as she was coming to think of him, gripped the babydoll in his meaty fists, and began to tug. It seemed as though everyone in the room, Jessica included, took a collective intake of breath as the material began to tear. The sound of the cheap fabric parting without resistance seemed indecently loud, as the nightdress was ripped in two from neckline to hem. Her breasts had already been as good as on show through the sheer nylon, but now they were revealed to all the watching eyes, defiantly bare. Jessica heard a vague murmur of appreciation among the men present, but, following the rules of this bizarre game, nobody openly verbalised their approval of her body.

While Cologne Man returned to his manipulation of her aching nipples, the man behind her raised the stakes a little further by slipping his fingers into the waistband of her panties. Splaying them out over her mound, he pressed the middle one between her already soaking pussy lips. He grunted, conveying his satisfaction at her finding her so wet.

When that thick digit began to move, flicking at her clit, Jessica found she no longer cared who he might be. Between his expert stimulation of her pussy, and Cologne Man's ruthless groping of her tits, she was being taken swiftly to the point of orgasm.

Jason must have recognised the signs, for he snapped, 'Ease back. Don't get the slut too excited. After all, I haven't decided whether she'll be allowed to come or not.'

She moaned. He almost never called her "slut" when they were alone, and he certainly didn't toss the word around in the casual way the other masters did when they addressed their submissive, but using it now, emphasising her role as a mere vehicle for the men's pleasure, only excited her further. She was his slut, she knew it, existing only to do his bidding, and that knowledge gave her the freedom to permit whatever might be done to her.

The fingers were withdrawn from her panties, and she bit back a whimper of disappointment. Again nylon ripped, as the waistband of the flimsy underwear came apart with one hard yank. The ruined garment was pulled out from between her legs; she couldn't see what he did with it, but the sound of gasps and raucous laughter suggested he'd held it up for them to view, and their reaction was to the sight of her juices. She could picture the way they shone against the sheer black fabric, and knew everyone in the room had seen the visible evidence of her excitement.

'Isn't it about time the men here got what they really wanted?' Jason asked. 'Down on your knees, Jessica.'

Being deprived of her sight made obeying a simple instruction all the more difficult. When she dropped slowly to the floor, her knee made contact with the sharp edge of the discarded belt buckle, and she yelped. Pulling it out from under her, she took a moment to surreptitiously explore its outline with her fingers. It reminded her of something; maybe, she thought, the horns of a cow. There was, she knew, more than one American here; perhaps one of them owned a cattle ranch, and that buckle symbolised his work, or his home state. Then she reminded herself she wasn't supposed to be looking for clues to anyone's identity, tempting though it might be. She was only here to serve.

A hard cock was presented to her mouth, and she swallowed it without protest. That familiar cologne lingered faintly in the hair at its owner's groin; perhaps he'd handled himself while he dressed, fantasising about what Jason Raynes's slut would be ordered to do to him, or perhaps he routinely spritzed down there.

He said nothing as she began to suck him, but his hips jerked, and his breath huffed out of him, harsh and fast. If she'd been close to the edge, he was even closer; when she slurped her tongue over his crown, he groaned and issued a muffled curse.

Buckle wanted in on the action too, for when she let the cock slip briefly from between her lips, his longer, thinner tool took its place. He tasted saltier, riper; unlike Cologne Man, he must not have washed before joining this little gathering. And a few experimental licks told her he wasn't on the same hair trigger as his companion.

She found herself falling into a rhythm, alternating between the two men, lapping at each in turn. All the time, she was aware of putting on a performance for whoever else might be watching, her master not least among them.

Soon, Cologne Man grew tired of only receiving half her attention. Grasping her hair in his fists, he held her head steady so he could thrust hard into the O of her parted lips. He fucked her mouth with short, fast strokes, hitting the back of her throat with each one and almost making her gag. Jessica drooled helplessly around his girth, nothing more than a receptacle for his desires. She'd never had anyone show less regard for her, but she knew without her he'd be reduced to bringing himself off with his own fingers. And that knowledge made her strong, even as he weakened her with the sheer force of his physicality.

His come shot out, too fast for her to swallow. It trickled out of her mouth, and down onto her chin. When he finally pulled away, she rocked back on her heels, coughing and spluttering. But she was allowed no respite; Buckle immediately took his place.

Around her, she heard the sounds of men shuffling from foot to foot, waiting their turn. Somewhere behind her, clothing hit the floor, and she wondered who might be getting naked. Was her master standing with his dick in his hand, stroking himself as he watched her sucking off Buckle? And did he, as she suspected, have the biggest cock of any man here, or would she be forced to take something even larger in her mouth, or her pussy?

For all his earlier sangfroid, Buckle was coming dangerously close to losing his load. Unlike Cologne Man, he didn't force the pace; if anything, he almost challenged Jessica to make him spend with the least amount of effort on his part. She laved him all the way from root to tip, covering every inch of his shaft with hot, slurping kisses, while her fingers toyed with his heavy balls. At last, when he began to show some emotion, grunting and trying to push himself a little deeper into her mouth, she stopped sucking him. Directing his cockhead in the direction of her breasts, she pumped his length hard in her fist, until she felt his spunk spatter her skin like warm rain.

Now her audience could have no doubt she'd brought both men to orgasm; the creamy trails on her face and breasts bore evidence to that. But still she didn't know who else she would have to please before her deliciously erotic ordeal was over.

The tense silence that had fallen on the room while Jessica made Buckle come was finally broken by Jason's voice. 'Very good, girl. You've performed beautifully so far. But that was only the beginning. Let us take a break for a moment, gentlemen.'

She heard a bottle being opened, and liquid sloshing into glasses, straining her ears for any clue as to how many drinks were being poured. Her intentions were thwarted when Jason came close to her, and pressed a glass to her lips.

'Drink this, my good girl.'

She burned under his praise, and the soft, lascivious

tone in which his words were delivered. If the men were drinking alcohol, all that passed her lips was water, cool and soothing to a throat made dry by her oral exertions.

'You're doing very well,' he told her. 'If anything, what you've done so far has exceeded my expectations. But let's get this off you, shall we?'

As he spoke, he pushed the torn nightdress from her shoulders. She let it fall to the floor, not caring what happened to it after that.

The other men seemed to have finished their drinks, for now someone else came to stand beside Jessica. Jason pressed a gentle kiss to the skin of her bare shoulder, then moved back to let the newcomer take centre stage.

Something was trailed over her body as she knelt up; she recognised the feel of soft suede as belonging to one of the toys in the pleasure chest Damon presented to all his guests. The flogger. Jason had whipped her with it before now, and it held little fear for her – at least when he wielded it. Who knew how this stranger might choose to use it?

Again she heard whispering, then Jason relayed the command. 'Get on all fours, and spread your legs a little way apart.'

Jessica did as she was told, knowing the position displayed her bottom, and the juicy contours of her sex. Footsteps paced around her, as though someone was taking his time to admire the view she presented. She tensed, having no way of knowing where the whip might land, or when. She took strength from knowing that her master watched from close by, like a ringmaster controlling events.

The flogger's tails swished through the air, fanning out as they landed on Jessica's rump. She sucked in a breath, but the blow had been gentler than she'd expected. It fell again, and a third time; whoever held the whip was moving his arm in a side-to-side motion, so the tails fell on first one buttock, then the next. He settled into a steady rhythm, using the flogger to create a steadily burning heat in her arse.

Close by, she heard a soft slapping, the sound of skin on skin, and realised someone must be wanking as he watched her being flogged. The feel of the whip landing on the tops of her thighs, catching the tender flesh there, brought her punishment sharply back into focus.

He knew what he was doing, building the pain with stroke after well-placed stroke. If Jessica had been able to see her backside, she knew the skin would be flushing red, the colour deepening each time the flogger made its stinging connection.

Now, a couple of strokes lashed the inside of each thigh, and though up till now she had been holding her posture without difficulty, she couldn't help reaching round to rub at the sore flesh.

'Jessica ...' Was that a hint of strain in her master's voice? Could he be the one who was pleasuring himself as he watched her being beaten?

'I'm sorry, master, but it hurts,' she said.

'It's meant to. Now hold still.'

She did her best to comply with the order as the flogger made contact with her arse again, landing on skin already well beaten. Gritting her teeth, keeping her limbs taut, she fought to ride out the pain, losing count of how many strokes she took before her mysterious punisher dropped the tool to the floor.

Jason gave her no further instruction, and all she could do was cast her head around, hoping to hear some clue as to what might be about to happen next – the ripping of a condom, or the sound of the drawer where the punishment implements were kept being pulled open again.

Instead, there was only silence, then the same rhythmic slapping she'd heard before, as an unseen fist shuttled along an erect cock. And was that a second hand, joining in with a rhythm that almost, but not quite, matched the first?

'Jessica, I want you to touch yourself.' Now there was no mistaking the hoarse quality to Jason's voice, as though forming the words was an effort. 'And I want you to tell me – tell everyone – what you're doing.'

When he'd asked her before, on their first night together, she'd been so reticent to comply. And it still embarrassed her to have to reach between her own legs, where her sex hung like a ripe, exotic fruit, and to say, 'I'm playing with my cunt, master. And I'm so wet and horny my juices are dripping down my legs.' But she did it, causing a collective groan of lust from the watching men.

Her fingers moved faster, as her need to come overrode all other impulses. Dimly, she was aware that two men were masturbating near to her, their lust driven and matched by her own. Someone grunted, and she heard an exclamation that might have been in Spanish. Then hot ropes of what could only be come landed on her arse. She felt a hand smoothing the creamy fluid into her skin, and the thought of how that must look, coupled with the teasing touch of fingers that could have belonged to any of the men at the resort, pushed her towards a sense-shattering orgasm. She had just enough presence of mind to shriek, 'Master, I'm going to come!'

'Do it, Jessica. Do it,' he urged her, and she almost lost her reason as the tension broke within her and she slumped to the floor, fingers still busily working in her sex as she climaxed.

Rolling over onto her back, she was greeted by another shower of come, splashing onto her breasts and belly. The groans that accompanied them had a familiar ring, and she knew without doubt it was Jason who had branded her with his essence.

Exhausted, she lay unable to move, while people moved around her. After a minute or so, the door opened and shut, and in the bathroom, the shower was turned on. Someone eased her gently into a sitting position, and the scarf was untied. When it was removed, she found herself staring into Jason's bluer than blue eyes, the look in them one that caused something to melt within her. More than admiration, it was the gaze of a man who clearly had deep feelings for the woman he regarded. Feelings she didn't particularly want to analyse right now.

She looked round, but they were alone, and nothing she could see in her immediate vicinity gave her any clues as to whose this suite might be.

'He's in the shower,' was all Jason would say, 'and he doesn't expect us to be here when he comes out. Let's go, Jessica.'

He took her hand, helping her to stand on legs that still trembled after everything she'd been put through.

As they left the room, closing the door silently behind them, she couldn't disguise the pride that swelled within her. She'd done everything Jason had asked of her, followed his every instruction, and pleasured a group of men on his command.

But still the question of which men she'd pleasured wouldn't go away. At least her stay at the resort was almost over, for she knew that for the rest of her time here she'd be looking at all the males she passed in the corridor, or sat with at dinner, wondering which of them had flogged her, and which had come over her tits ...

Jason pushed open the door of his room. 'Let's get you clean, you dirty girl,' he said, and led her in the direction of his bathroom.

Chapter Sixteen

'So, is submission everything you'd thought it would be?' Honey asked, propping herself up on one elbow and winking at Jessica.

'That depends on who's asking,' Jessica replied. She'd been expecting another session of discipline training on her last morning on the island, but instead Jason had said he wanted to spend some time on the beach.

'After all,' he'd said with a grin, 'how will anyone know I've been on holiday if I don't come home with a tan?'

She thought his skin looked appealingly sun-kissed already, but she hadn't said anything, relishing the chance to pretend, however briefly, that this was nothing more than a standard week in the sun, rather than some kind of kinky boot camp for those in need of lessons in submission.

'And if you're good,' he'd added, 'I might even let you have a dip in the hot tub.

That, she had to admit, did sound like something worth being on her best behaviour for, though she knew she wouldn't be able to go anywhere near the infinity pool without thinking about how close she'd come to losing her life in those innocuous-looking waters.

Now, Jason lay on a sun lounger to her left side, reading a day-old English newspaper that had been brought over with a delivery of supplies on an early-morning boat. 'I see United won again,' he commented to no one in particular, as he studied the sports pages.

'I have to say you look like you're enjoying yourself here,' Honey continued. 'You have a certain glow about you, Jessica, like you're getting something you've wanted for a long time.' She smiled. 'It's the look I get whenever Ray comes home with one of those cute blue Tiffany boxes.'

'So where's your master at the moment?' Jessica asked, seeing no sign of Rafael anywhere. Normally, he liked to hover close enough to pick up on Honey's latest indiscretion, and dish out whatever punishment he felt it merited. She was finally beginning to understand the strange dynamic that existed between them, with Honey deliberately provoking her master into disciplining her, and both of them gaining a thrill from her brattish behaviour.

'Oh, he's gone to play golf, with Damon, my darling Ray and that hottie, Sebastian. I did worry that they might want to take me along, but this is strictly a boys-only outing. They're probably discussing business, or measuring their dicks in the forest, or something. It's just as well. There's nothing I find more boring than golf.'

As if Honey had invoked the men's presence simply by mentioning their names, Sebastian Voller came into view, bounding down the steps that led to the beach, followed by Rafael dos Santos.

'Apologise to her,' Sebastian was saying. 'Tell the little slut why her master is nothing but a big, fat *Verlierer*. A loser.'

'Someone seems pleased with themselves,' Jason muttered, folding his newspaper shut and sitting up on the lounger.

'Let's just say we had a little wager on who would go round the course in the fewest strokes ...' Sebastian took a wad of Damon dollars from his breast pocket, and fanned his face with them. 'I'm so hot, I need a drink to cool down. Come on, why don't you let me buy you one?' he said to Jason. 'Or, rather, let Mr I Can't Play Golf here buy them.'

Jessica could see Honey already mentally planning the taunts she would throw at her master about his lack of ability on the golf course, in return for a serious bottom-warming. She marvelled at the way the woman could turn any situation into a potential opportunity to be spanked.

'No thanks,' she heard Jason say. 'It's kind of you to offer, but it's a little early for me to be drinking, to be honest.'

'But I insist,' Sebastian replied. 'Let me buy you something without alcohol. I need to celebrate my good fortune.'

Obviously sensing that the German would keep on at him till he accepted, Jason said, 'OK then, mate. Lead the way.'

He rose from the lounger, and beckoned Jessica to follow him. As they headed in the direction of the bar, Jessica could already hear Honey saying, 'You mean to tell me you couldn't even beat him at a simple game of golf?'

'That slut's mouth will get her into trouble,' Voller commented, though he too clearly knew that was the whole point of Honey's mockery.

The barman greeted them with a smile as Sebastian and Jason settled themselves on high-backed stools. The man's grin seemed especially wide as he turned it on Jessica, and she found herself blushing. Had he been one of the mystery men who'd watched her yesterday? Might he have been the one who'd flogged her? She shook her head, sure she was reading too much into his friendly demeanour.

'What can I get you?' he asked.

'I'll have a beer,' Sebastian began, 'and my friend will have a –?'

'Grapefruit juice, thanks,' Jason supplied.

'A grapefruit juice. And give the slut a glass of sparkling water.'

Jessica couldn't quite decide how she felt about being included in Sebastian's largesse. She couldn't help remembering how Max had reacted when the man had beaten him to that business deal; nothing really got Max down for long, but he'd been quite bitter about the whole affair, claiming some kickback must have been involved. And Jason didn't seem to trust the man for some reason. But, she reasoned, this was just a drink. What harm could it do?

Except one drink turned into two, and then a third, and the conversation between Sebastian and Jason, which was initially light-hearted and friendly and mostly concerning football and rock music, took a sudden turn.

'I'm in the mood for another wager,' Sebastian

declared. 'You see, Jason, I have no hard feelings about the fact you beat me in the bidding for Jessica here, but I would really relish the opportunity to show you the kind of discipline I would have given her had I been her master.'

'And what kind of discipline is that?' Jason asked, keeping his tone light, though Jessica could sense something in Sebastian's words had rattled him.

'Real discipline. The kind that is meant, my friend, not the kind that is merely played at. And I suggest a little game of chance to see whether or not I will be permitted to give her that discipline.'

As he spoke, Max wandered into the bar, deep in conversation with Wesley Cole. Simone, Cole's slave, walked a couple of paces behind them. She wore a collar around her neck, and from the wide metal ring set into the front of the collar hung a thin, crook-handled cane. Whether this had just been used on her, or was just about to be, Jessica couldn't tell, though the girl's careful posture suggested she might be recovering from a recently striped bottom.

'Ah, just the man!' Sebastian announced, beckoning the newcomers over. 'Max, my friend, I am just about to engage Jason here in a wager. I am proposing that we use a coin to decide who gets to punish her. We toss it, and whoever calls heads or tails correctly, best out of three, will have the chance of inflicting discipline on that beautiful bottom of hers. What do you say, Jason?'

Jason glanced over at Jessica. She kept her expression neutral, not wanting to let him know about the shiver of alarm that had passed through her at Sebastian's talk of "real discipline". In one of their discussions on the subject, Jason had told her no master should attempt to inflict punishment on a submissive if either one of them had been drinking heavily, or was under the influence of drugs. But though the German had been drinking, she could tell he was nowhere near the recklessly drunk stage; if anything, she suspected the alcohol had only sharpened his desire to beat her.

'OK, you're on.'

'Good man.' Sebastian fished in his pocket, and dug out a coin. 'Heads or tails?' he asked Jason.

'Heads,' Jason replied at once.

'And so you leave the tail for me. How appropriate.'

He flipped the coin, and let it land on the bar counter, covering it with his hand. Everyone crowded round to see how it had fallen. Jessica felt her stomach lurch with disappointment at the sight of the reverse side of the coin, with its pattern of a galleon in full sail. But that's only the first one, she told herself. Still two chances for it to land Jason's way.

Again Sebastian tossed the coin; this time, the Queen's head stared back at them when he pulled his hand away.

'So, it all comes down to the final throw,' he commented. 'I am sure we are all of us hoping that our luck is in.'

Jessica couldn't help wondering if he included her in that remark. Max too, given the animosity between her husband and Voller. The tension in the little group gathered at the bar had risen a notch or two; even Simone, who had no stake at all in the proceedings, gave Jessica's arm a sympathetic squeeze. Everyone knew how much was riding on this third toss of the coin.

Sebastian strung the moment out as long as he could. Had he taken a sneaky look at the outcome before announcing the result to everyone? If so, he gave nothing away; Jessica knew she would never want to play poker against him.

'And the coin comes down –' He moved his hand away with a flourish, giving everyone a moment to look and take in what Jessica was sure he already knew. 'Tails. I am sorry, Jason. What can I say?' His smile, like his words, carried not a hint of sincerity.

'So now what?' Jason asked.

'We take Jessica to the dungeon.' Sebastian motioned to the barman. 'You keep a few bits and pieces behind the bar, don't you?'

'Yes, sir,' the man replied.

'Well, would you be so kind as to lend me a collar and leash? My friend here has been so incredibly lax in his enforcement of discipline as to neglect to keep the slut on one.'

'Of course, sir.' The barman disappeared from sight below the lip of the counter for a moment, returning with a black studded collar to which a dog leash had already been clipped. Sebastian fitted it in place around Jessica's neck, fastening the buckle a notch tighter than anything she had experienced with Jason. The thick leather pressing against her throat made her acutely aware of every breath she took, and reminded her that he could, if he wished, restrict her air intake even further.

'Come with me, slut,' he ordered, giving the leash a sharp tug. 'And whoever else cares to witness her discipline ...'

He cast a look around the little group. Wesley Cole

shook his head. 'I'd love to, but I've got an arse of my own to stripe before the morning's out.'

His words, and the urgency with which they were delivered, reminded Jessica that she and Max weren't the only people who would be leaving the resort today. Others were taking in the opportunity to fit in one last punishment session, one last enactment of a cherished fantasy, before returning to the pace and pressure of their everyday life.

That left Jason and Max, neither of whom appeared to want to leave her alone with Voller. The small party set off for the dungeon at a swift pace, Sebastian taking long strides that forced Jessica to scurry to keep up with him, or risk being choked by the tightly buckled collar.

'You have the dungeon key already?' Jason asked as Sebastian opened the door to the small, low-ceilinged room, no doubt remembering how he'd had to book it out from the reception desk.

'Let's just say I had a feeling this would be my day.' Sebastian smiled, ushering Jason and Max inside.

He dragged Jessica into the centre of the room, bypassing the whipping stool and the pillory. If he didn't intend to fasten her to either one of those, then what? She stood still, trying to show no emotion, as he went to a chest that contained various pieces of equipment, and pulled out a length of thick, industrial-looking chain. A wide, sturdy eyebolt had been screwed into the ceiling; Sebastian pulled over a small step stool that had been provided for the express purpose of allowing the dominant to feed chain, or rope, through that eyebolt, leaving the ends dangling down. Once he'd done that, he buckled a thick cuff round each of Jessica's wrists, and fastened those cuffs to the ends of the chain. She was left with her arms stretched tautly above her head, and her feet just about planted on the floor. It was a position she felt she could hold for a short amount of time before the strain on her shoulders became too painful, and she hoped he didn't plan to leave her there for an extended session.

Max and Jason were standing to her left, just in her line of sight. She didn't turn her head to look at either one of them, afraid to meet their gaze in case she broke down and begged to be freed. She couldn't embarrass either her husband or her master like that, even though every fibre in her body screamed that she really didn't want to be at Voller's mercy.

'You don't know how long I've wanted to have you like this,' Sebastian told her, making a slow, appraising circuit of her naked body. 'Bound and helpless, about to learn what it truly means to submit. And you will submit, as you never have before.'

For the first time since they'd entered the dungeon, Jason spoke up. 'Before you go any further, you need to know that she has a safeword. It's "violets".'

'Safewords are for amateurs,' Voller scoffed. 'I will know when the slut has taken enough, I assure you, and it will not be when she thinks that's the case.'

Jason stepped close to Sebastian, and Jessica could see his hands were bunched into tight fists. 'She has a safeword,' he repeated, his voice a low hiss, 'and if she uses it and you don't stop what you're doing, trust me, I will knock your teeth right down your throat.'

Max put a hand on Jason's shoulder, pulling him away from the other man. 'It's OK.'

'No, it's not, Max. Sebastian thinks he knows what's best for Jessica, but he doesn't. She's not Simone, or one of the house girls who's used to being disciplined all the time. She's not a pain slut, and I don't want him treating her like she is.'

Sebastian said nothing, merely turned and studied the rack of implements on the wall. To Jessica's anguished eyes, he seemed to take for ever to make his choice. At last, he selected a riding crop, and she shuddered inside. Could he have known that was her least favourite out of everything Jason had used on her, with its vicious bite and the fiery lines of pain it left in its wake?

'One last thing before we begin ...' Holding the crop between his teeth, Sebastian undid his shirt buttons, and took it off. Despite herself, Jessica felt a traitorous trickle of juice escape from her pussy at the sight of the German stripped to the waist. His muscles were nearly as spectacular as Jason's, his skin tanned an even golden shade, and his pouting good looks reminded her irresistibly of the coat check boy at Envied. How long ago it seemed now that she had pinned that guy up against the wall of his own cloakroom and fucked him to a standstill. Had it really been little more than a week? So much had happened since that night, and it had brought her to a place where a man with the same model looks but the temperament of a true sadist was about to thrash her with a riding crop.

She composed herself as best she could, as Sebastian took the crop in his hand and stepped up to where she hung in her bonds. He trailed the leather keeper over her body, using it to circle each of her nipples in turn.

'You have glorious breasts, slut,' he told her, 'but

they would look so much better with a ring through each nipple. If you were mine, I would have rings in your pussy lips too, so I could padlock them together if I chose, and make sure no one played with your cunt except me. Not even you, slut.'

Jessica glanced down, not wanting to see the expression on his face as he outlined all the things he would do to her body, as if she really was nothing more than his possession. Almost without meaning to, her gaze settled on his crotch, and the bulge that strained against the fly of his skin-tight jeans. Not as big as Jason's, but still a nice size, enough to make her feel it as he stretched her pussy walls apart …

'But there are other things that can be done to your nipples,' Sebastian continued. He moved away for a moment, to rummage in another drawer. When he returned, he held two small metal objects that reminded Jessica of the bulldog clips she'd used in her secretarial days. Even though his words had already let her know how he intended to use them, she couldn't prepare herself for the bite of the first clip as he attached it to her nipple. Losing her composure, she cried out, the chain that held her in place rattling as she jigged from foot to foot in an attempt to lessen the pain.

'Stay still, slut,' Voller ordered her, fixing the second clip to her other nipple. Again, it pinched like fury, and she did her best to bite back her cry of anguish.

'Clips here too, I wonder?' Sebastian cupped the mound of her pussy, and she shook her head, eyes wide with fear. Surely he couldn't mean to fasten those cruel metal jaws to her soft nether lips? She'd never be able to take the pain. His touch became more sensual, causing her to relax into the feeling of having her clit stroked. Then he stepped away. She almost screamed at him not to go back to the drawer. Her alarm was unnecessary; he merely licked his fingers with relish, lapping up the wetness that had transferred to them as he'd fondled her.

'She tastes so delicious. Like the finest of wines,' he commented. 'And I'm sure the prospect of punishment has only heightened her bouquet. She wants this, Raynes, whatever you might say. She wants me to thrash her. And what the slut wants, the slut gets.'

With that, he walked round behind her. He was out of her line of vision, but she could smell his aftershave, surprisingly light for such an avowed dominant, and hear the soft squeak of his leather boots as he moved. He played the crop over her buttocks, acquainting himself with their contours.

'I will not ask you to count the strokes, nor will I let you know how many you are to receive. That, as you are by now well aware, is at my discretion – and mine alone.' That last remark had to be directed at Jason. He didn't react, though Jessica could tell her master was itching to pluck the crop from Sebastian's fingers.

Through all this, as the two men had circled each other, each trying to assert that his method of discipline was the right one for her, Max had stood watching. What did her husband have to say about all this – if he had to choose, would he prefer that she be beaten by Jason, who knew and respected her limits, or Sebastian, who wanted to take her well beyond the threshold of what she'd so far endured? By not stepping in, or attempting to sway the German from his course of action, she supposed he'd made his choice. Well, she would take everything Sebastian had to give; she would show Max how well she could suffer, and she would make him – and Jason – proud of her.

Her resolve almost crumbled to nothing when the crop slashed down on her backside for the first time. Sebastian didn't hold back; he put the full force of his arm behind the stroke, and she yelled at the top of her lungs as a bolt of fire sizzled through her punished cheek. A second stroke fell, on the other cheek, and she cried out again.

'Make as much noise as you like,' Sebastian said. 'These walls are thick. No one can enjoy the music of your cries except us.'

He really did enjoy making her scream; it was clear in his voice. Sebastian considered himself a master craftsman, and the evidence of his skill would be the marks his crop left on her skin.

Without giving her pause, he striped her arse again and again, each line running parallel to the ones he had left already. Hot torment flooded her body, every blow increasing her anguish. She writhed in her bonds, wishing there was some way to escape from the agony he was inflicting on her, and knowing that she had nowhere to go. Her arms were beginning to ache, tears spilled from her eyes, and she knew already that the sea journey on the little boat that would take them back to St Thomas and their connecting flight to Antigua would be a most uncomfortable one.

Sebastian altered his line of attack, slashing at her thighs. Again, the strokes were placed with precision, coming down on the places where the skin was softest and most vulnerable. How many had she taken in total?

A dozen? More? All she knew was that it felt like he'd been beating her for ever.

She looked over to Max and Jason. Her husband's expression could only be described as pure lust, as he drank in the sight of her punishment, and she wouldn't be at all surprised to find his cock hard as iron in his underwear. Jason, meanwhile, seemed torn between anxiety and frank admiration – for her fortitude, not Voller's skill with the crop, she was certain.

Aware that her attention had wandered elsewhere, Sebastian brought the focus sharply back to him by coming round to stand in front of her. The pain in her clamped nipples had subsided to a dull throb, almost forgotten as she fought to cope with the fearful hurt in her buttocks and thighs.

He used the tip of the crop to flick one of the pinching little clips. Even that gentle touch was enough to waken the fire in the aching bud. Repeating the action on her other nipple, he smiled at her sobbing plea not to hurt her further.

'I knew you'd be beautiful when you begged,' he said, running his finger down her cheek to wipe away a stray tear. Like her master, he had the ability to switch from cruelty to tenderness in a heartbeat, and her body responded as it always did when Jason showed her kindness; her pussy fluttered and she realised that pain had begun to meld with pleasure. 'Beg me now, slut, beg me to whip you till you come.'

'No, please ...' He couldn't mean that, surely? She'd taken so much, and there had been moments when the safeword had hovered close to her lips. He couldn't intend to carry on with her cropping.

'Beg me,' he repeated, sliding his fingers into her pussy and using two of them to fuck her with slow in and out movements. 'Do what I tell you, because where I give pleasure, I can also give pain.'

The crop slashed down, almost without her being aware of it, and caught her squarely on the left breast. She squealed in pain, even as her pussy muscles clutched possessively at his invading fingers.

'Where shall I strike you next?' he asked. 'The other breast, or maybe –'

He pulled his fingers out of her gripping hole, and ran the crop's keeper over her mound and down into the cleft between her lips. His intention was unmistakable.

'God, no, please!' she cried. 'You can't – please!'

'You know I can do whatever I want. You could use that special word my friend here seems so keen on – and such pretty flowers they are too – or you can take your punishment like a good girl.'

Those words, the ones her master always used when she had truly pleased him, seemed so wrong coming from Sebastian's lips. From somewhere, she conjured up the last of her defiance. 'Only my master can give me permission to come.'

'Is that so?' Sebastian brought the crop down on her right flank, then her left. She looked over at Jason, eyes full of mute appeal, knowing that his intervention could bring this to an end.

'Yes, it is,' he said, voice strong and steady. 'And I give you that permission, Jessica. Come for me. Come like you never have before.'

To Jessica, pushed beyond endurance by the pain of the clips and the crop and the strain in her bound limbs, it seemed that even before Sebastian whipped the flesh at the apex of her mound, her orgasm took her. It spiralled her up to a place where nothing and no one could touch her, pain and pleasure fusing into something deep and sweet and all-consuming. She babbled nonsense as she came, racked by spasms that set the chains rattling and dancing all over again, and then she was being freed from her restraints and pulled into Jason's arms.

Of all the men in the room, it somehow felt right that he was the one who held her close, soothing her as she came slowly back to awareness of her surroundings.

'You did so well,' he told her, 'but it's not quite over yet.' With that, he removed the clips, and she almost cried out again as sensation began to flood back into her tormented nipples. He bent his head, and suckled each of the sore buds in turn. 'That better?' he asked her as he straightened again.

'Yes, thank you. Thank you for everything, Jason.'

Their eyes met, and their lips followed, as she kissed him with all the passion she had, not caring that her husband stood only a couple of feet away. So much emotion in one kiss, she thought as they finally broke apart. Lust and desire and need and want. And beneath it all, the acknowledgement that this was goodbye, and it would never happen again. If things were different, she could really fall in love with this guy. She tried to ignore the little voice in the back of her head that told her she already had.

It left only the formalities to be concluded. Jason went to shake Max's hand. 'It's been an honour and a privilege to own your wife,' he said, 'and now she's all yours. She'll do whatever you ask of her, and if she doesn't –' he grinned '– well, I think you know how to deal with her now.'

'Thank you, Jason,' Max replied. 'I couldn't have wished for a better man to tame Jessica.'

Jason turned to Voller, who paused in the act of shrugging on his shirt. 'And Sebastian, mate, I've learnt a few things from you about how to treat a submissive. I just don't think I'll ever be putting them into practice.'

With that, he strode from the room, leaving Jessica to throw herself into her husband's arms and feel the closeness of his body for the first time since they'd left London.

Chapter Seventeen

'I think you and I need to talk.'

Max looked down at Jessica as she lay on the big bed in his suite. He'd taken her there once they'd left the dungeon, and now he was rubbing a soothing salve into the welts that Sebastian Voller's crop had left on her arse. As gentle as he tried to be, she winced at his touch, and he could almost curse the man for having inflicted such a brutal punishment on her, if it wasn't for the fact the sight of Jessica writhing and sobbing beneath the blows had excited him beyond belief. He was still hard, his cock aching for relief.

Jessica rolled on to her side, clearly trying to find a position that was comfortable for her. 'Talk? About what?'

'What happened just now, mostly.' He took a breath, wondering best how to begin. 'Jess, when I brought you out here, I wasn't totally convinced I was doing the right thing. I thought you might rebel the moment you found out what kind of place this really was, and demand to go home. But you didn't. And I'm so proud of you for staying, and submitting to everything that's been done to you.'

'I needed it, Max.' Jessica linked her fingers with his.

'And even a couple of weeks ago, I would never have thought that, but I've learnt now that there's a part of me that responds to being kept in line.'

'And I've learnt a few things about myself this week too. Mostly that I get turned on by watching another man discipline you. Even an arrogant, self-centred bastard like Voller. If he'd demanded that you suck his cock after he'd whipped you, or wanted to fuck your arse, I wouldn't have objected. I'd have enjoyed the sight. In fact, that's the one thing I'd have liked to do more of this week, watch you service some other guy.'

'So you weren't in whichever suite it was yesterday, when I was blindfolded and having to suck two men off at once?' Jessica asked.

'No, I wasn't, and when we get home I'm going to make you tell me every last filthy detail of what you did to them.' He sighed wistfully. 'That's the one thing Damon should do to make this place even better. Install digital recording equipment in all the rooms, so guests could have mementos to take home ...'

He stopped, aware that he was getting side-tracked from his main point. Though that didn't stop thoughts flashing through his mind of what Jessica might have looked like, on her knees and paying attention to two hard, jutting cocks.

'But there's still one thing I need to know. It's been eating away at me for a couple of days now, ever since I saw you at Damon's table the other night, and with everything that happened just now ...' Max couldn't stop himself blurting out the words. 'Are you in love with Jason Raynes? Because I'm pretty damn sure he's in love with you.'

'Max, I ...' This time, when Jessica's eyes met his, tears glistened in their green-gold depths. 'I have very strong feelings for him, I can't deny that. After everything that's happened between us this week, it would be almost impossible for me not to.'

Max snorted. 'Are you sure? Because I look at a woman like Honey Forrester, and she seems to treat everything that's done to her as one big game.'

'But that's how she operates. She deliberately winds up whoever's dominating her by not taking anything seriously, because she knows he'll react by punishing her. I'm sure she loves her husband, just as I love you.'

'That still doesn't answer my question.'

Jessica sighed. 'You're the man I married, Max. You're the man I promised to love and obey for the rest of my life, and when you spanked me after you brought me back from Envied, I realised just how much that promise meant to me. But Jason pushed buttons I didn't even know I had, and he showed me what being properly mastered is all about. You've watched him, you've watched the other men here; you can treat me the same way, I know you can.'

'That's as may be, but –'

She put a soft finger to his lips, cutting him off. 'If you and I weren't together, then yes, I would give myself to Jason. He stirs things in me that no one else ever has, apart from you. And he might not be the pretty toy boy you fought so hard to keep me away from, but he's so right for me in so many ways. All of which are completely immaterial, because after today I'm never going to see him again, am I?'

Max pulled Jessica up till her face met his, and they

kissed. How long had it been, he wondered as he tasted the softness of her mouth, since he'd held her in his arms and kissed her quite so thoroughly? And why had it taken the fear that he might lose her to another man to rouse him to this peak of passion?

'God,' he murmured, when they came up for air, 'I've done so many things, seen so many things this week, and when it comes down to it, what I want to do more than anything else is make love to my wife? How vanilla is that?'

'There's nothing wrong with good old vanilla sex,' Jessica said, watching him as he began to shed his clothes. 'We just know now that it's more important for us to keep things spicy.'

He tossed his shirt to the floor, conscious that they didn't have much time. In just over an hour, they would need to check out and make their way down to where the boat would be berthed, waiting to take them off the island. His shorts and underwear followed. So much to do; his bags still needed to be packed, and someone would have to collect Jessica's things from her room ...

No, he told himself, let that wait. This is more important. If this week has taught us anything, it's that we can't get back into the habit of relegating sex to the last in a list of chores.

Conscious of finding a position that would be comfortable for Jessica and her punished arse, he rolled her onto her side, and slotted in behind her. As he guided his cock to her entrance, he heard her give a murmur, and wondered if he'd accidentally placed his weight against some sore spot.

Instead, she said, 'And if anything will stop you

feeling jealous, just remember Jason was never able to fuck me without a condom. He's never felt what you feel right now.'

She was right; there was no barrier shielding him from the hot, velvet interior of her cunt, nothing to prevent this most intimate of connections. And though he usually preferred to be able to look into her eyes as he fucked her, this felt right, to be spooning with her, his leg draped over her hip and his cock sliding into her with slow, shallow thrusts. Jessica pushed her rump back at him, a little gingerly, and the self-imposed restriction of her movements sent a wicked thrill through him. In future, if the marks of a punishment were emblazoned on her arse as he fucked her, it would be because he had placed them there. Or he would take her pussy, or her arse, while he had her in bondage, feeling her strain in her restraints beneath him as his cock ploughed into whichever hole he chose.

Yet something still pricked at him; the faint, almost suppressed tone of disappointment in Jessica's voice when she'd talked about never seeing Jason again. He'd already confessed to her how exciting he found it when she was forced to pleasure another man – or woman, given the state he'd been in when watching her undergo her "customs examination" at the hands of Delice Abrams. Would he gain anything by making sure she was exclusively his, as he'd intended to do by bringing her here to learn what it meant to be tamed – or would he simply end up the loser?

He could hardly follow his own train of thought, as his need to come grew more desperate and the pace of his thrusts into his wife's beautiful body increased.

Somehow, he managed to blurt out, 'It doesn't have to be the end.'

'What do you mean?' Jessica asked, her own fingers buried in her cunt as she sought to match her orgasm to his.

'You and Jason. It doesn't have to end when we all leave the island.' Then the come surged from his balls, flooding into Jessica's strongly convulsing body as she came a moment behind him, and for a moment nothing mattered as he emptied himself.

When he finally rolled away from her, fighting the urge to sleep that usually followed good sex, the plan returned to mind, in sharper focus than before. He reached for the phone, and when the receptionist picked up, he asked her to put him through to Jason Raynes' suite.

Jason stood at the side of the bed, taking inventory in his mind of everything he'd brought with him to make sure he left nothing behind. He'd emptied the closet of his clothes and footwear, and the bathroom of his selection of toiletries, along with the half-finished complimentary bottles of shampoo and shower gel. If nothing else, when he used them, he would remember how Jessica's body had smelled when she'd used those same products.

The contents of the toy chest were his to take away too: the flogger, the silken ropes, the lube and healing salve. He'd packed those deep in the bottom of his bag; souvenirs of the most unforgettable week of his life, and the woman he'd created those sweet memories with.

It had almost broken his heart to watch her walk out of the room with Max's arm around her, after she'd orgasmed under the lashes of Voller's riding crop. So strong, so brave, so beautiful; she truly was his perfect submissive. He would search for a long time before he found anyone who came close to her. But he had to let her go; he'd taken on the task of training her on her husband's behalf, and he'd done it to the best of his ability. Though he still saw flashes of the wilful cougar who had apparently driven her husband to distraction, they only served to help make her the complex woman who presented so much more of a challenge than a brat like Honey or a compliant pain slut like Simone.

Give it a few weeks, he told himself, and all this will seem like some kind of dream; something to distract yourself while you're ordering another overweight, out of shape businessman to do another set of 20 press-ups. Move on, and let her go, however painful it is.

He was in the process of zipping up his carry-on bag, ready to go downstairs and check out, when the phone rang. Expecting to hear the voice of a receptionist, reminding him that he needed to be on his way very soon, he found himself instead being greeted by Max Sheringham.

'Wait for me in reception when you've checked out,' Max said. 'I'll be with you in ten minutes or so. Don't worry, they won't let the boat go without us.'

'What's all this about, Max?'

'Let's just say I have a proposition for you. One I think you'll be very interested in.'

Epilogue

'Display!'

Automatically, Jessica dropped to the floor, facing the front door, linked her hands behind her head, and spread her thighs wide to reveal her pussy. The position had become second nature to her, and she no longer needed Max's approving murmur to let her know she'd adopted it to his satisfaction.

In the three weeks since they'd returned from Isla Barada, Max had begun to assert his dominance over her. One of his rules was that she should be waiting in the hall, naked and in the display position, ready for his return home. On a number of occasions, he'd walked in with Mickey in tow; the first time this had happened she'd felt a flush of embarrassment at the driver seeing her so completely exposed, but the sweet thrill of humiliation had overtaken her, and now she felt almost disappointed if Mickey wasn't around to admire her body and flash the wolfish grin that let her know how much he'd enjoy the privilege of being allowed to use her mouth, or her tight pussy. She had the feeling it wouldn't be too much longer before her husband granted him that privilege.

Today was different, though: Max hadn't been to his office, or spent the day in one dull, interminable business meeting after another. Instead, he'd been hard at work in his study upstairs, ploughing through sales projections and sheaves of figures, pondering whether to make a bid to outfit a chain of upmarket health clubs with a new lighting system. She'd spent most of the day taking him one cup of coffee after another, and now Jessica was required to display herself because a guest would shortly be arriving.

'Jason rang me when he got to Kew Bridge Station. He should be here any minute now.'

Sometimes, she had to pinch herself to make sure this was real, and that Max and Jason really had come to an arrangement. Waiting for the moment Jason would ring the doorbell, announcing his presence at their home, her mind drifted back to the day they'd left the island resort. Jason had been waiting for them in reception, clearly baffled by Max's talk of a proposition, and as one of the boat's crew had carried their bags down to the beachside berth, Max had put a companionable arm around Jason's shoulders and begun to outline what he had in mind.

It was, he'd explained, an unorthodox arrangement. He didn't know whether it was usual in the BDSM lifestyle for a submissive to have one full-time master and another who took on domination duties whenever it might be required, but that was his proposal. As he freely admitted, he still had much to learn about disciplining a wayward wife; even here, where one could play out a scene – or any number of scenes – 24 hours a day, he still felt like he'd only scratched the surface. Which was where Jason's expertise came into play.

Jessica had held her breath, waiting for Jason's response. Would he contemplate such an outrageous suggestion, or would he decide he wanted nothing more to do with the couple? She prayed he wouldn't walk away, knowing she needed him in her life, not only to guide Max but to give her the loving chastisement she supplied so masterfully. Anxious moments had passed before he'd finally nodded and said he'd be delighted to help Max keep her in line.

She remembered little of the journey back to London. The boat ride had caused her some discomfort; she'd spent most of it kneeling on the floor of the boat, as that had been the position which placed the least pressure on her welted bottom. She'd been relieved Voller was staying on the island for another week; he'd have taken smug satisfaction from knowing she was still suffering the after-effects of her cropping, though she doubted he'd have been quite so pleased if he knew what Max and Jason had been plotting between them. The German might have bested Max in the boardroom, but she knew which one of them she would rather have as her lord and master.

The flight from St Thomas to Antigua had been short and uneventful, and when they'd arrived at V.C. Bird airport, Max had used his charm on the girl on the check-in desk to persuade her to upgrade Jason to a first class seat alongside theirs. As they'd boarded the plane Jessica had kept an eye out for Darragh, remembering their antics in the bathroom on the flight out, but he wasn't part of the crew. Instead, they'd been looked after by a solicitous, slightly matronly blonde, who'd kept them supplied with champagne. Jessica supposed Jason had made the most of his surroundings, but she'd fallen asleep somewhere over the Atlantic, and only woken as the Surrey countryside began to become visible through gaps in the cloud cover.

Mickey had been waiting for them once they'd cleared customs at Gatwick, and Jason had accepted Max's offer of a lift back into the centre of London. If the chauffeur wondered who the Sheringhams' travelling companion might be, and why he and Max each had a hand high on Jessica's thigh as the car sped along the Westway, he was discreet enough not to say anything. He'd certainly learnt enough about their arrangement – and Jessica's new role as Max's submissive, as well as his wife – to satisfy any curiosity since then.

Max and Jason had exchanged numbers, and Jason had made a promise that he'd be round to discipline Jessica very soon. Except work commitments on the parts of both men had meant he'd only been in contact with her via phone and text message since then. Deeply filthy text messages, she had to admit, in which he told her exactly what he intended to do to her the next time he had her naked and bound before him. They'd stoked the fires of her imagination, so that now, as she waited for him to walk through the door, she was already wet in anticipation of his first command.

The doorbell sounded, and Max went to let their visitor in. Jessica's heart beat a crazy tattoo in her chest. What if it wasn't Jason, but some charity collector, or local council official, checking whether their property was in need of loft insulation? The thought she might find herself exposing her wet, spread pussy to some spotty young jobsworth with a clipboard alarmed her –

and stoked the same feelings of shame and arousal that fuelled her desire to submit.

To her relief, Jason strode into the hallway. He must have come straight from a training session, as he wore a hooded top, which he pulled off to reveal a sleeveless muscle vest, and cycling shorts that clung to his thick thighs and outlined his cock, not yet hard but every bit as enticing as Jessica remembered.

'Max, it's good to see you, mate,' he said, clapping Max on the back as the two embraced like old friends. 'And Jessica – just as lovely and obedient as ever.'

'The position comes naturally to her now,' Max replied, referring to Jessica in the dispassionate fashion that never failed to excite her further. 'And her training's coming along nicely in other respects.'

'Well, I'll need to make sure of that. Have you been keeping a list of her demerits, like I asked?'

'Oh yes, and they've certainly been mounting up. In fact, she received her credit card bill this morning, and I'd venture to suggest that her spending is in danger of getting out of control.'

Jason shook his head. 'We can't have that kind of behaviour, now can we? What do you reckon, Max? She's swapped the thrill of prowling for young flesh for the thrill of flashing the cash in Harvey Nicks?'

The two had fallen into an easy companionship, their minds running on a parallel track which Jessica knew was destined to lead to some kind of punishment for her. She might have objected if her pussy wasn't already clenching with need. The need to feel a warming hand on her bottom; the need to be penetrated by a hard, thick cock as the reward for taking her punishment.

'And you've set up a punishment room in the house, as I suggested?' Jason asked.

'Well, I discipline her in my study, but it's the perfect environment. I'm having a whipping stool delivered next week, one that I can keep stowed in a cupboard up there till I need it. You'll have to come round and see it when it's in place.'

'So –' Jason stalked in a slow circle round Jessica as he spoke, and she knew he was admiring her naked body, and the submissive posture in which she continued to hold herself, from the back as well as the front '– what were you planning on using to discipline her today?'

'I've been thinking about it, and she hasn't actually had the cane used on her as yet. Damon supplied me with a nice, thin, whippy one, but I thought I'd take some guidance from you as how best to lay the strokes on. I've a feeling it's an instrument that requires a little more delicacy than the paddle.'

'You're right there, Max.' The grin on Jason's face told Jessica just how much he would enjoy imparting this particular lesson in discipline.

'Jessica, come with us!' Max barked out the order, and she rose to her feet. The two men began to lead the way upstairs, where the cane waited, and punishment would be applied in the manner they felt best. Revelling in her newfound status as submissive slut to the two men she loved best in the world, she knew she wouldn't want it any other way.

Also from Xcite Books

Students of Submission
Leigh Turner

Sally becomes one of eight university students hand-picked to participate in a financially rewarding social psychology experiment. At a secluded mansion, she meets the imperious "Director", Jane, who is to subject them to a series of challenges, more sexual than social. She realises she must hide some details of her recent history from Jane, but can she do this in the face of the increasingly perverted violations which rob her of will, as she succumbs more with each deliciously inventive pleasure, increasingly in thrall to the dominant older woman and her well versed staff?

ISBN 9781908766298
Available July 2013

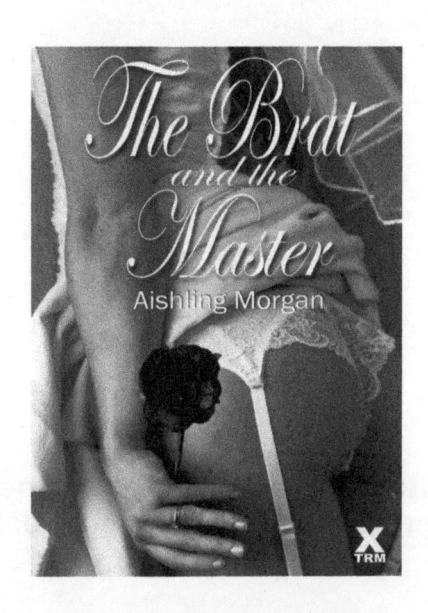

The Brat and the Master

Aishling Morgan

The 100th novel by popular erotic author Aishling Morgan.

Set in London's extraordinary world of fetish and sadomasochism, where love goes hand in hand with cruelty and obsession, *The Brat and The Master* is an erotic novel for modern times.

More reality than fantasy, Jasmine, the Brat, and Adam, her master, will be familiar to some and disturbing to others as Aishling explores the dark underbelly of human sexuality

ISBN 9781908766946

Xcite

Xcite Books help make loving better with a wide range of erotic books, eBooks and dating sites.

www.xcitebooks.com
www.xcitebooks.co.uk

facebook

Sign-up to our Facebook page for special offers and free gifts!